NICOLAS DICKNER

N I K O

L S K I

A NOVEL

Translated by Lazer Lederhendler

ALFRED A. KNOPF
Canada

PUBLISHED BY ALFRED A. KNOPF CANADA

Copyright © Éditions Alto, 2005
English Translation Copyright © 2008 Lazer Lederhendler
Published by arrangement with Éditions Alto, Quebec City, Quebec, Canada

Library and Archives Canada Cataloguing in Publication

Dickner, Nicolas, 1972–
[Nikolski. English]
Nikolski / Nicolas Dickner ; Lazer Lederhendler, translator.

Translation of: Nikolski.
ISBN 978-0-676-97879-7

I. Lederhendler, Lazer, 1950– II. Title.
PS8557.I325N5313 2008   c843'.6   C2007-905096-4

First Edition

Text design: CS Richardson

Printed and bound in the United States of America

2 4 6 8 9 7 5 3 1

For Mariana Leky — N.D.

For Chana (Anya) Lederhendler, née Andruzewska — L.L.

1989

Magnetic Anomaly

MY NAME IS UNIMPORTANT.

It all started in September 1989, at about seven in the morning.

I'm still asleep, curled up in my sleeping bag on the living-room floor. There are cardboard boxes, rolled-up rugs, half-disassembled pieces of furniture, and tool boxes heaped around me. The walls are bare, except for the pale spots left by the pictures that had hung there for too many years.

The window lets in the monotonous, rhythmic sound of the waves rolling over the stones.

Every beach has a particular acoustic signature, which depends on the force and length of the waves, the makeup of the ground, the form of the landscape, the prevailing winds and the humidity in the air. It's impossible to confuse the subdued murmur of Mallorca with the resonant roll of Greenland's prehistoric pebbles, or the coral melody of the beaches of Belize, or the hollow growl of the Irish coast.

The surf I hear this morning is easy enough to identify. The deep, somewhat raw rumbling, the crystalline ringing of the volcanic stones, the slightly asymmetrical breaking of the waves, the water rich in nutriments—there's no mistaking the shores of the Aleutian Islands.

I mutter something and open my left eye a crack. Where can that unlikely sound be coming from? The nearest ocean is over a thousand kilometres away. And besides, I've never set foot on a beach.

I crawl out of the sleeping bag and stumble over to the window. Clutching at the curtains, I watch the garbage truck pull up with a pneumatic squeal in front of our bungalow. Since when do diesel engines imitate breaking waves?

Dubious poetry of the suburbs.

The two trash collectors hop down from their vehicle and stand there, dumbstruck, contemplating the mountain of bags piled on the asphalt. The first one, looking dismayed, pretends to count them. I start to worry; have I infringed some city bylaw that limits the number of bags per house? The second garbageman, much more pragmatic, sets about filling the truck. He obviously couldn't care less about the number of bags, their contents or the story behind them.

There are exactly thirty bags.

I bought them at the corner grocery store—a shopping experience I'm not about to forget.

Standing in the cleaning-products aisle, I wondered

how many garbage bags would be needed to hold the countless memories my mother had accumulated since 1966. What volume could actually contain thirty years of living? I was loath to do the indecent arithmetic. Whatever my estimation might be, I was fearful of underestimating my mother's existence.

I went for a brand that seemed sufficiently strong. Each package contained ten revolutionary ultraplastic refuse bags with a sixty-litre capacity.

I took three packages, for a total of 1,800 litres.

The thirty bags turned out to be adequate—though I did on occasion enlist my foot to press the point home—and now the garbagemen are busy tossing them into the gaping mouth of the truck. Every so often, a heavy steel jaw crushes the trash with a pachyderm-like groan. Nothing at all like the poetic susurrations of the waves.

Actually, the whole story—since it needs to be told—began with the Nikolski compass.

The old compass resurfaced in August, two weeks after the funeral.

My mother's endless agony had worn me out. Right from the initial diagnosis, my life had turned into a relay race. My days and nights were spent shuttling from the house, to work, to the hospital. I stopped sleeping, ate less and less, lost nearly five kilos. It was as if I were the one struggling with the tumours. Yet the truth was never in doubt. My mother died after seven months, leaving me to bear the entire world on my shoulders.

I was drained, my thinking out of focus—but there was no question of throwing in the towel. Once the paperwork was taken care of, I launched into the last big cleanup.

I looked like a survivalist, holed up in the basement of the bungalow with my thirty garbage bags, an ample supply of ham sandwiches, cans and cans of concentrated frozen orange juice and the FM radio with the volume turned down low. I gave myself a week to obliterate five decades of existence, five closetfuls of odds and ends crumbling under their own weight.

Now, this sort of cleanup may seem grim and vindictive to some. But understand: I found myself suddenly alone in the world, with neither friends nor family, but still with an urgent need to go on living. Some things just had to be jettisoned.

I went at the closets with the cool detachment of an archaeologist, separating the memorabilia into more or less logical categories:

- a cigarillo box filled with seashells
- four bundles of press clippings about the U.S. radar stations in Alaska
- an old Instamatic 104 camera

- over three hundred pictures taken with the aforementioned Instamatic 104
- numerous paperback novels, abundantly annotated
- a handful of costume jewellery
- a pair of Janis Joplin–style pink sunglasses

I entered a troubling time warp, and the deeper I plunged into the closets, the less I recognized my mother. The dusty objects belonging to a life in the distant past bore witness to a woman I'd never known before. Their mass, their texture, their odour seeped into my mind and took root among my own memories, like parasites. My mother was thus reduced to a pile of disconnected artifacts smelling of mothballs.

I was annoyed by the way events were unfolding. What had started out as a simple matter of sweeping up was gradually turning into a laborious initiation. I looked forward to the time when I would finally reach the bottom of the closets, but their contents seemed inexhaustible.

It was at this point that I came upon a large packet of diaries—fifteen softcover notebooks filled with telegraphic prose. My hopes were rekindled. Maybe these diaries would allow me to put together the pieces of the puzzle?

I arranged the notebooks chronologically. The first one began on June 12, 1966.

—

My mother headed off to Vancouver when she was nineteen, feeling that a proper break with one's family should be gauged in kilometres, and that her own falling-out deserved to be measured in continents. She ran away one June 25, at dawn, in the company of a hippie named Dauphin. The two confederates shared the cost of gas, shifts at the wheel, and long drags on thin joints rolled as tight as toothpicks. When not driving, my mother wrote in her notebook. Her script, very neat and orderly at the outset, quickly started to furl and unfurl, tracing the eddies and whorls of THC.

At the beginning of the second notebook, she had woken up alone on Water Street, barely able to stutter a few halting phrases in English. Notepad in hand, she went about communicating through ideograms, by turns sketching and gesturing. In a park, she made the acquaintance of a group of arts students who were busy crafting delicate origami manta rays out of psychedelic paper. They invited her to share their overcrowded apartment, their cushion-filled living room and a bed already occupied by two other girls. Every night at about two a.m., the three of them squeezed in under the sheets and smoked hand-rolled cigarettes while they discussed Buddhism.

My mother swore she would never return to the East Coast.

Whereas her first weeks in Vancouver were recounted with a wealth of detail, the rest of her journey grew more and more elliptical as the demands of nomadic life evidently supplanted those of narration. She never stayed anywhere more than four months, but would all of a sudden take off to Victoria, then Prince Rupert, San Francisco, Seattle, Juneau and a thousand other places she did not always bother to identify clearly. She scraped by thanks to various paltry expedients: hawking poems by Richard Brautigan to passersby, selling postcards to tourists, juggling, cleaning motel rooms, shoplifting in supermarkets.

Her escapade went on like this for five years. Then, in June 1970, we showed up at the Vancouver central station with two huge duffel bags just about bursting at the seams. My mother bought a train ticket to Montreal, and we crossed the continent in reverse, she curled up in her seat, me nestled in the depths of her uterus, an imperceptible comma in an as yet unwritten novel.

When she got back home, she briefly made up with my grandparents—a strategic truce aimed at securing the endorsement she needed from them to buy a house. In short order, she purchased a bungalow in Saint-Isidore Junction, a stone's throw from Châteauguay, in what was to become the southern periphery of Montreal, but which at the time still retained something of the countryside, with its ancestral houses, its fallow land and its impressive population of porcupines.

Now saddled with a mortgage, she had to take work in Châteauguay—at a travel agency. Paradoxically, this job put an end to her youthful roving, and to her diaries too.

The last diary ended on an undated page, *circa* 1971. I closed it, deep in thought. Of all the omissions that punctuated my mother's prose, the most important was Jonas Doucet.

Nothing was left of that transient sire but a stack of postcards scribbled with indecipherable handwriting, the final one dating back to 1975. I had often tried to crack the secret of those cards, but there was no way to make sense of their hieroglyphics. Even the postmarks were more revealing, as they limned out a path that began in southern Alaska, went up to the Yukon, then back down again toward Anchorage, and ended in the Aleutians—more precisely, on the American military base where my father had found employment.

Under the pile of postcards was a small, crumpled box and a letter from the U.S. Air Force.

I learned nothing new from the letter. The box, on the other hand, illuminated a forgotten pit in my memory. Now totally flat, it had once contained a compass that Jonas had sent me for my birthday. That compass came back to me in astounding detail. How could I have forgotten it? It was the only tangible proof of my father's existence, and had been the pole star of my childhood, the glorious instrument with which I'd crossed a thousand imaginary oceans! Which mountain of debris was it buried under now?

I combed the bungalow from top to bottom in a reckless frenzy, emptying drawers and cupboards, searching behind the sideboards and under the rugs, crawling into the darkest recesses.

It was three in the morning before I tracked it down, stuck between an aquarium-sized deep-sea diver and an apple-green garbage truck, at the bottom of a cardboard box perched on two rafters in the attic.

The years had not improved the appearance of the poor compass, a five-dollar gizmo most likely found near the cash register of an Anchorage hardware dealer. Luckily, its lengthy proximity to metallic toys had not demagnetized its needle, which persisted in pointing (what seemed to be) north.

Strictly speaking, it was a miniature mariner's compass, composed of a transparent plastic sphere filled with a clear liquid in which there floated a second, magnetized and graded sphere. The inclusion of one sphere inside another, as in a tiny matryoshka, guaranteed a gyroscopic stability that could withstand the worst storms: no matter how strong the waves might be, the compass would lose neither its bearings nor the horizon.

I fell asleep in the attic with my head sunk in a cumulus of candy-pink insulation, the compass resting on my forehead.

—

Superficially, that old compass seems perfectly unremarkable, just like any other compass. But on closer examination one realizes that it doesn't point exactly north.

Some individuals claim to be aware at all times of precisely where north is located. However, like most people, I need a marker. When I'm sitting behind the bookstore counter, for example, I know magnetic north is located 4,238 kilometres away, in a beeline that runs through the Mickey Spillane shelf and goes to Ellef Ringnes Island, a pebble lost in the immense Queen Elizabeth archipelago.

But, instead of pointing toward the Mickey Spillane shelf, my compass lines up 1.5 metres to the left, right in the middle of the exit door.

It is true, of course, that the planet's magnetic field is subject to local distortions, and that north can appear to be a little out of place. There are several possible reasons for this anomaly: an iron ore deposit in the cellar, the upstairs neighbour's bathroom plumbing, the wreck of a transatlantic liner buried under the pavement of St-Laurent Boulevard. Unfortunately, none of these theories is borne out by the facts, because my compass points to the left of north no matter where I happen to use it. This raises two troublesome questions:

- What is the cause of this magnetic anomaly?
- Where (the hell) is the compass pointing to?

Common sense would suggest that my imagination constitutes the main local anomaly of the magnetic field, and that I'd be better off tidying up rather than daydreaming. But anomalies are like obsessions: all resistance is futile.

I vaguely recalled my geography courses: magnetic declination, the Tropic of Cancer, the pole star. It was time to put this buried knowledge to use. Equipped with a pile of geography books and an assortment of maps of various scales, I set out to determine exactly where my compass was pointing.

After some painstaking calculations, I arrived at a declination of 34° W. Following that bearing, one crossed the Island of Montreal, Abitibi and Temiskaming, then Ontario, the Prairies, British Columbia, the Prince of Wales archipelago, the southern tip of Alaska, a bit of the North Pacific, and the Aleutian Islands, where one finally landed on Umnak Island—more specifically, on Nikolski, a minuscule village inhabited by thirty-six people, five thousand sheep and an indeterminate number of dogs.

One could therefore deduce that the compass pointed toward Nikolski, an answer that struck me as rather satisfactory, even though it had the disadvantage of clouding the issue instead of elucidating it.

Nothing is perfect.

From time to time a customer will ask me what that weird amulet is around my neck.

"It's a Nikolski compass," I reply.

The customer, not understanding, smiles and politely changes the subject. He asks, for instance, where he might find books by Mickey Spillane.

As you may have guessed, I don't work in a geographical institute or a store that deals in globes.

In point of fact, S. W. Gam Inc. is a business entirely devoted to the acquisition, presentation and retailing of the previously owned book. In other words, a second-hand bookshop. Mme Dubeau, my esteemed employer, hired me in the fall of my fourteenth year. At the time, I earned a measly $2.50 an hour, a wage that I graciously accepted so that I might survey all these books from on high with no further obligation than to read.

I've been working here for four years now, a span that appears a good deal longer to me than it is in reality. During that time, I dropped out of school, my mother died and my few childhood friends vanished. One of them took off to Central America at the wheel of an old Chrysler and has not been seen since. A second one is studying marine biology in a Norwegian university. There's been no news of him. The others have simply disappeared, swallowed up by the course of events.

As for me, I'm still parked behind the bookstore counter, where, however, I get to enjoy a spectacular view of St-Laurent Boulevard.

My job is more like a calling than a normal career. The silence is conducive to meditation, the wages are consistent with a vow of poverty and, as for my work tools, they're in keeping with a sort of monastic minimalism. No hi-tech electronic cash register; all the calculations are done manually—old-fashioned sums scratched on whatever scrap of paper is to hand. No computerized inventory, either; I'm the computer, and I have to recall on demand the last place I glimpsed, for example, that Esperanto translation of *Dharma Bums*. (Answer: In behind the pipes of the washroom sink.)

The work is not as simple as it may appear; the S. W. Gam Bookshop is one of those places in the universe where humans long ago relinquished any control over matter. Every shelf holds three layers of books, and the floorboards would vanish altogether under the dozens of cardboard boxes, but for the narrow, serpentine paths designed to let customers move about. The slightest cranny is put to use: under the percolator, between the furniture and the walls, inside the toilet tank, under the staircase, even the dusty closeness of the attic. Our classification system is strewn with microclimates, invisible boundaries, strata, refuse dumps, messy hellholes, broad plains with no visible landmarks—a complex cartography that depends essentially on visual memory, a faculty without which one won't last very long in this trade.

But it takes more than a good pair of eyes and a few ounces of memory to work here. It's crucial to develop a particular perception of time. The thing is—what's the best way of putting this?—that different avatars of our bookshop coexist simultaneously in a multitude of discrete times, separated by very thin ellipses.

This warrants some explanation.

Each book that enters here can meet its next reader at any moment in the history of the shop, in the future as well as the past. Whenever Mme Dubeau sorts a new shipment of books, she repeatedly consults her version of the *Encylopaedia Britannica*—some thirty notebooks where she records all special requests made by clients since February 1971—to see whether, ten years before, someone may have been looking for a title among the freshly arrived books.

From time to time she grabs the telephone with a triumphant smile.

"Mr. Tremblay? This is Andrée Dubeau at the S. W. Gam Bookshop. I have some good news. We've just received *The History of Whaling in Fairbanks in the Eighteenth Century*!"

At the other end, Mr. Tremblay represses a shiver. Here he is, abruptly transported back to the pristine icebergs that haunted his nights throughout the heat wave of 1987.

"I'll be right over," he mumbles feverishly, as if he'd been reminded of an important appointment.

Mme Dubeau crosses out the request and closes the *Britannica*. Mission accomplished.

I can't leaf through those thick notebooks without trembling a little. There is no other occupation that provides as accurate a measure of the passage of time—a number of the clients recorded in those pages are long dead. Some aren't the least bit interested in the books anymore; others have moved to Asia without leaving a forwarding address—and many will never find the book they so coveted.

I wonder if there may not somewhere be a *Britannica* of our desires, a comprehensive repertory of the slightest dream, the least aspiration, where nothing would be lost or created, but where the ceaseless transformation of all things would operate in both directions, like an elevator connecting the various storeys of our existence.

Our bookshop is, in sum, a universe entirely made up of and governed by books—and it seemed quite natural for me to dissolve myself in it completely, to devote my life to the thousands of lives duly stacked on hundreds of shelves.

I have sometimes been accused of lacking ambition. But might I simply be ailing from a minor magnetic anomaly?

Here we are, nearly at the end of the prologue.

It took me two weeks to fill the thirty bags that the garbage collectors pitched into their truck this morning.

One thousand eight hundred litres of ultraplastic—thirty years of living. I've kept only the strict minimum: a few boxes of souvenirs, some furniture, my personal effects. The bungalow is up for sale and a couple of buyers seem interested. The transaction should be finalized within a week.

By then I'll already be somewhere else, in my new apartment in Little Italy, just opposite the statue of old Dante Alighieri.

The garbagemen have finished their work and are mopping their foreheads, wholly oblivious of the story they've just taken part in. I watch the truck effortlessly chew up the bags and swallow whatever was left of my mother.

The end of an era; I find myself in virgin territory, without signposts. I look around nervously. The Nikolski compass is lying on the floor near the sleeping bag, forever indicating 34° W. I slip its cherry-red strap around my neck.

The garbage truck drives away. In its wake, the moving van arrives.

Grampa

NOAH WAKES UP WITH A START.

Everything in the trailer is quiet. He hears nothing but the noise of a car travelling down the road. Curled up in her sleeping bag, Sarah is softly breathing in the lower bunk. He rolls over on his side, hoping to get back to sleep, but can no longer find a comfortable position. And yet this narrow bunk seemed so vast to him when he was five years old. Now not a night goes by without him garnering a bump on the skull or a bruised elbow.

So he struggles in silence, looking for that comfortable position, only to find after a few minutes that he is fully awake. Sighing, he decides to get up, noiselessly climbs down the ladder, pulls on a T-shirt and a pair of jeans.

Two Chipewyan Indians are seated at the kitchen table. Their long white hair is braided and their hands are wrinkled. Noah doesn't know their names. One is his great-great-grandfather. As for the other . . . not the faintest idea. Very little is known about them, except that they lived and died in northern Manitoba at the end of the nineteenth century.

Noah greets them silently and goes out.

The trailer is anchored in the middle of forty million hectares of rye shrouded in a fine mist, which is punctured here and there by a few electricity poles. The sun is still below the horizon and the air smells of wet hay. The rumble of a tractor can be heard in faraway spurts.

Noah walks barefoot to the edge of the field. A thin thread of water runs at the bottom of the irrigation ditch. The pungent tang of diazinon blends with the scent of clay—familiar fragrances.

Just as he starts to unbutton his fly, he hears a pickup truck approaching on the road. Hands on hips, he cuts short the procedure. An old red Ford comes into view, rushes past, speeds off toward the west. When it is far enough away, Noah sends a long stream of urine shimmering into the ditch.

Walking back to the trailer, he reflects on this peculiar display of modesty. He can't shake the unpleasant feeling that the vehicle was encroaching on their territory, as if Route 627 actually ran through their bathroom.

On close examination, that image isn't so very far from the truth.

For years, when asked where he'd grown up, Noah would sputter some vague response—Saskatchewan, Manitoba, Alberta—and swiftly change the subject, before any more questions were raised about this shadowy taboo.

Rare indeed were the individuals to whom Noah would eventually disclose the true (though unlikely) story of his mother, Sarah Riel.

The starting point was the summer of 1968, when she left the reservation where she had been born, near Portage la Prairie. She was sixteen and about to marry a certain Bill, who was from Leduc, Alberta. More often than not, his skin disappeared under a sheen of crude oil, but no one was fooled by the camouflage; the man was white—actually a little pink around the joints—and by marrying him Sarah lost her Indian status, and the right to reside in a reservation.

The full significance of this administrative nicety loomed up ten months after her wedding, when Sarah bolted from her conjugal abode with a black eye, a garbage bag hastily stuffed with clothes and the firm intention never to look back. She *borrowed* Bill's car and trailer and began to roam between the Rockies and Ontario, in step with seasonal employment.

When the Department of Indian Affairs introduced certain amendments to the Indian Act seventeen years later, Sarah could have claimed her Indian status. But she never did go through the required process; she had gotten so used to the road that enclosing herself in a reservation was unthinkable.

Anyway, she liked to reiterate, she would never let a bunch of civil servants decide whether or not she was Indian. True, her family tree did include a few French-speaking offshoots, but anywhere beyond three generations back there were only old Indian nomads, forced by treaty to settle down, then confined to countless reservations with exotic names like Sakimay, Peepeekisis, Okanese, Poor Man, Star Blanket, Little Black Bear, Standing Buffalo, Muscowpetung, Day Star or Assiniboine.

A half-dozen of these elders still haunted the trailer, seated for all eternity at the star-studded Formica-top kitchen table. These serene, speechless ghosts would watch the landscape roll by, and wonder where the hell all the buffalo had gone.

Noah's father, for his part, hailed from the distant shores of the Atlantic. He came from an Acadian family of the Beaubassin area, headstrong settlers whom the British had deported to the four corners of the American colonies: Massachusetts, Carolina, Georgia, Maryland, New York, Pennsylvania or Virginia.

Noah enjoyed the contrast between the two branches of his genealogy, the paradox of being the descendant of both the reservations and a deportation. His enthusiasm, however, was based on a misperception, because his ancestors had not in fact been deported. Like many Acadians, they had absconded a short while before the *Grand Dérangement* to seek refuge in Tête-à-la-Baleine, an isolated village on the Gulf of St. Lawrence, past the reach of any road.

It was this secluded place that, two centuries later, would witness the birth of Noah's father, Jonas Doucet.

He was the seventh offspring of a bountiful family: eight brothers, seven sisters, five cousins, two uncles, an aunt, a pair of grandparents—in total, three generations of Doucets crammed together in a tiny cabin. He had been baptized Jonas, a stroke of luck, as the biblical repertory might have inspired names with a less agreeable ring, like Elijah, Ahab or Ishmael.

You grew up quickly in that lost corner of the continent, and at fourteen Jonas was already slinking about in the port of Montreal, some eight hundred nautical miles upstream from his native village. He hired onto a wheat freighter bound for Cuba, with the round trip scheduled to take less than three weeks. But Jonas changed ships in the port of Havana and hopped aboard a cargo leaving for Trinidad. A third cargo took him to Cyprus. From Cyprus he crossed the Suez Canal headed for Borneo, and from there he went on to Australia.

Sailing from one port of call to the next, Jonas rounded the globe a dozen times. As the harbours came and went, he moved up the ranks, from the kitchen to the engine room, then from the engines to the radio.

After a few years as assistant, he earned his licence and became a full-fledged radio operator.

Jonas enjoyed this curious profession halfway between electronics and shamanism, where the operator conversed with the upper atmosphere using what, for the uninitiated, was an obscure rhythmic language. Taking on the shaman's role did, however, involve certain hazards; the old sparks—those who stayed at the switch for too many years—often suffered from an irreversible atrophy of the vocal cords. They could be seen mouldering in portside taverns, looking like jaded griots, incapable of communicating other than by tapping out bursts of Morse on their beer mugs.

That prospect gave Jonas pause, and he decided to settle down on terra firma.

He glanced around nervously as he stepped ashore in the port of Montreal, ten years after his departure. During his absence, Quebec had been shaken in quick succession by the death of Premier Maurice Duplessis, the FLQ Crisis, the modernization of Montreal, Expo 67 and the sexual revolution. What he discovered was a far cry from the mariner's life or the industrial hurly-burly of port cities, and especially from the Quebec of his memories, which added up to fourteen years of squalor in a tiny village on the Lower North Shore.

As soon as his foot touched the ground, Jonas was overcome by a bizarre malady: he could no longer

move about on steady ground. Old sea dogs are familiar with this balance disorder, which comes from
being too long exposed to the rolling of the sea. There
is no cure for land sickness except to ride it out for a
few days, while the inner ear naturally grows accustomed to the situation. Still, Jonas was worried; the
days went by and the horizon kept on tilting. When he
sat down, the dizziness would knock him off his chair.
When he stood up, the nausea would send him puking
over the guardrails. When he lay down, he would
flounder back and forth across the bed like a channel
buoy, and wake up trussed in his sheets.

After two weeks of this queasy regimen, he resolved
to apply a radical remedy that would either save him or
slay him: he would cross the continent solo.

While this exploit may seem trivial, it's worth
recalling that for Jonas the shortest line between
Montreal and Vancouver now ran through the Panama
Canal. Nevertheless, he hiked his duffel bag onto his
shoulder, went out, green-faced and wobbly, and stuck
his thumb in the air along Highway 40.

A week later, Jonas found himself alone on a back
road in Manitoba, sweating profusely, stretched out on
the gravel, waiting in vain for the nausea to subside. He
had vomited the contents of his stomach tenfold and,
between two heaves, berated himself for not having put
to sea again. To think that at the very moment he could
be navigating on the northern Indian Ocean, gently

tossed by a monsoon storm, with his forefinger on the telegraph key . . .

High in the sky, a covey of interested vultures glided directly overhead. He closed his eyes, ready to let himself die of thirst and dizziness. When he opened them again five minutes later, Sarah was there, proffering a canteen of tepid water.

It was *Grampa*'s easy rolling that restored Jonas to life.

Grampa was a 1966 Bonneville station wagon, wider than it was long, its beige paint peppered with rust spots and its radio refusing to pull in anything but country music on the AM dial. The wheezy motor of this ocean liner, prematurely used up by tens of thousands of kilometres of trailer duty, made it impossible to exceed fifteen knots except when running before the wind. This road-bound vessel, which had never seen anything but flatland and more flatland, somehow knew how to feign to perfection the swell of the sea. Perhaps its shock absorbers had been manufactured near the Atlantic? Perhaps its weary tires had been salvaged from the sides of a tugboat?

Whatever the case, the simulated rolling rescued Jonas. He breathed more easily, the nausea faded and the giddiness went away, so that within a few hours the dying man, saved from sunstroke at the eleventh hour, metamorphosed into Corto Maltese.

That evening, Sarah invited Jonas to move into the

silver-coloured trailer. It should be said that she'd been rambling for nearly two years, and the loneliness had been at times hard to bear. So Jonas wanted to make it to the other coast? No problem. The crossing could be bartered for a little company.

The couple was fated to last for only 1,500 kilometres. No more was needed.

In late August they reached the eastern outskirts of Fort Macleod, Alberta, at the fork in the highway. Route 2 ran north, in the direction of Calgary. Route 3 climbed toward a bluish vanishing point in the Rockies. Sarah pulled *Grampa* over on the shoulder of the road and summed up the situation:

"The Pacific is that way, straight ahead."

Jonas hiked his bag onto his shoulder once again, took a deep breath, vaulted over the Rockies, changed river basins and plunged into Vancouver headfirst, amid the torrential rains that then enveloped the Pacific Ocean.

Noah made his entrance nine months later.

Legend has it that he drew his first breath in Manitoba, somewhere between Boissevain and Whitewater, near the railroad tracks, in a spot that, according to the road maps, is located at the exact geographic centre of Canada. The truth is that it was the exact centre of nothing at all: an immense forest of spruce stretched to the east, blackish peat bogs to the north. To the south, the Turtle Mountains, and to the west, a plain that appeared to end in China.

One thing was certain—the nearest ocean was two thousand kilometres away.

However unlikely this may seem, Noah learned to read from road maps.

Sarah had appointed him chief navigator, a job that involved keeping an eye on the cardinal points, the magnetic north and, incidentally, the contents of the glove compartment. He therefore spent the long prairie hours exploring that tight space smelling of dust and overheated plastic. Besides small change, unpaid traffic tickets and cookie crumbs, it contained dozens of road maps: Ontario, the Prairies, the Yukon, North Dakota, Montana, the West Coast and Alaska. *Grampa*'s glove compartment enclosed the entire known universe, carefully folded and turned in on itself.

Over the years the maps had become almost transparent, riddled with little gaps along the seams. By dint of deciphering this paper topography, Noah came to understand the alphabet, then words, sentences, paragraphs. *Road Information*, *Federal Picnic Grounds* and *Weather Broadcast* were the first words he was able to read. Sarah soon added the names of some Indian reservations—such as Opaskwayak, Peguis or Keeseekoowenin—while pointing out which of his great-great-uncles or second cousins lived there. Strangely, she never suggested they go visit their invisible kin. Noah did not press the point. His family tree was, like everything else, a transient thing that receded with the landscape.

The day came when the maps were no longer enough to slake Noah's curiosity, and he turned to the only tome in the family library: a battered book forgotten by Jonas when he had left in haste.

The book had followed an unimaginable trajectory. After several decades on the shelves of the library of the University of Liverpool, it had been stolen by a student, been passed from hand to hand, escaped two fires and then, left to its own devices, returned to the wild. It had crossed thousands of kilometres in various bags, travelled amid the cargo in damp crates, been thrown overboard but continued on its way in the acidic belly of a whale, before being spat out and retrieved by an illiterate deep-sea diver. Jonas Doucet finally won it in a poker game in a Tel Aviv bar one intemperate night.

Its pages were brittle, spotted with countless small rust-coloured specks, and if you buried your nose in it you could detect vegetation patiently endeavouring to colonize the depths of the paper. Not only was this Noah's one book, but it was also one of a kind, bearing a host of distinctive signs. In the middle of page 58, for instance, there was a large, brownish bloodstain. Between pages 42 and 43 a fossilized mosquito had made its home, a tiny stowaway flattened by surprise. And scribbled in the margin of page 23 was the mysterious word *Rokovoko*.

It was called the Book with No Face, because its covers had been torn away since the dawn of time. It was a kind of anthology of sailors' yarns, whose first page reproduced a map of the Caribbean that never ceased to amaze Noah. How could such a mass of water coexist with such a small amount of land? It resembled a negative of the map of Saskatchewan, where there was a lake for every island, and oceans of grain instead of the sea.

The Prairies gave way to shipwrecks, sordid tales of pirates and the promise of yellow gold buried beneath distant coconut trees. The book was written in English and French, and sprinkled with bizarre nautical jargon and archaic expressions. Noah refused to be impressed. Though terms like Wa-Pii and Moos-Toosis escaped his grasp, nothing could prevent him from tacking among royal sail rudders, main topsail hatchways, and assorted bowline tackle.

It took him nearly a year to get through the Book with No Face, and that heroic reading left an indelible imprint on him. Never again would he be able to separate a book from a road map, a road map from his family tree, or his family tree from the odour of transmission oil.

Sarah and Jonas Doucet exchanged letters for several years. Their correspondence constituted a massive tongue stuck out at the most elementary logic, since

Jonas, like Sarah and Noah, never stayed put very long. After spending a few months in Vancouver, he once again headed north, constantly travelling from village to village, from job to job, working his way up the West Coast toward Alaska, never very far from the sea. Meanwhile, Sarah and Noah zigzagged across Saskatchewan, stopping to work in Moose Jaw, before returning to the suburbs of Winnipeg for the winter.

The combined effect of these two vagrancies made any exchange of letters highly improbable, and Sarah had to develop a special postal system.

When the time came to mail a letter, she spread the road maps of western North America out on *Grampa*'s hood and tried to guess where Jonas might be. For example, if he had just spent a number of weeks in Whitehorse, she figured she could pin him down in Carmacks. Then she would change her mind; Carmacks was too far from the sea. Instead, Jonas would continue along Route 1 toward Anchorage, and was probably about halfway there. She therefore addressed the letter to General Delivery in Slana, and put down Assiniboia General Delivery by way of return address, as she planned to be passing through there in the next few weeks.

With any luck, Jonas would receive her letter and send a postcard to Assiniboia; otherwise, the envelope would be lost in the void and Sarah would chalk up a miss on the road maps.

Plain common sense dictated that not a single missive sent out according to this hare-brained system would ever reach its target. Nevertheless, year in, year out, they managed to exchange a letter a month. This *32* absurd correspondence lasted until the arrival of a mysterious postcard. Thirteen years later, Noah would still recall that day in minute detail.

They had stopped in Mair, a hamlet huddled around the parking lot of a thresher-harvester dealer. In the middle of the village, the three usual institutions marked out an equilateral triangle: the farmer's co-op *(Founded in 1953)*, the post office (SOC ORI) and Brenda's Restaurant *(Today: Fish n' Chips, Dessert, Beverage, $3.95)*.

Having cast a suspicious eye on the restaurant's menu, Noah and Sarah crossed the road in the direction of the post office.

In any one year, they would visit several hundred post offices, and Noah never tired of these brief stopovers. He loved the glint of the steel postal boxes, the worn counters, the faded posters celebrating the subtle joys of stamp collecting and, more than anything, the air of those rooms, redolent with crushed paper, ink stamps and the rubbery aroma of elastic bands.

While he soaked in the atmosphere of the post office, Sarah asked the clerk if a letter had come for them. The old man took out the box containing the letters addressed to Mair General Delivery—undoubtedly one of the planet's most underused addresses—and was amazed to find a postcard in it. He examined it unhurriedly before finally turning it over to see who the addressee was.

"Sarah and Noah Riel, right? Got any ID?"

As Sarah fished about in her pockets for an old health insurance card—she never had owned a driver's licence—he nonchalantly studied the postcard. Noah, clutching the edge of the counter, stamped his feet impatiently and with mute rancour eyed the ungainly clerk's burgundy tie and yellow, nicotine-stained moustache. As soon as Sarah presented her ID, Noah snatched the postcard from the man's fingers and darted toward the exit.

Sarah caught up with him on the stairs of the post office, where he sat in the dust contemplating their thirty-five-cent miracle. The picture on the postcard showed a humpback whale in full flight, huge fins spread wide, a thirty-ton bird striving in vain to break loose from its element. In one corner of the photo, the graphic designer had added *I Love Alaska* in red italics. On the reverse side, Jonas had scrawled three rambling sentences that Noah tried unsuccessfully to decode— mainly because he was as yet incapable of reading anything except the words printed on a road map. Instead, he fell back on the stamp, which bore a seashell striped with the post office seal.

He cast a questioning glance at Sarah: "Nikolski?"

They eagerly opened the map of Alaska on *Grampa*'s scorching hood. Noah's finger slid down the index, found the coordinates for Nikolski—E5—traced a long diagonal across the map and stopped on the island of Umnak, a remote chunk of land in the endless vertebral column of the Aleutians, far off in the Bering Sea.

He circled in blue ink the tiny village of Nikolski, at the western tip of the island, and then stepped back to survey the map in its entirety.

The nearest road ended at Homer, eight hundred nautical miles to the east.

"What on earth is Jonas doing there?!" Noah exclaimed, raising his arms skyward.

Sarah shrugged. They folded the map and went on their way without saying anything more.

After Nikolski they received no more postcards from Jonas. Sarah continued to write regardless, believing this was merely a turn of bad luck, but the months passed, the post offices filed by and the radio silence persisted.

There were a number of hypothetical explanations for Jonas's silence, the most plausible being that the fragile miracle of their correspondence had run its course and that each letter exchanged throughout the years amounted to an intolerable loophole in the immutable laws of chance, which had quite simply regained their sovereignty.

But Noah had the stubborn personality of a six-year-old nomad, and couldn't be bothered with the immutable laws of this or that. Fixing his gaze on the horizon, he mulled over many kilometres of grim thoughts, trying to imagine what in the world Jonas might be concocting in Nikolski. He must have become infatuated with an Aleutian girl and was trying to start a new life by obliterating all his previous endeavours. Noah imagined a flock of slant-eyed half-brothers and half-sisters, grubby little village-dwellers who might be monopolizing his father's attention.

He repeatedly proposed to Sarah that they pay Jonas a surprise visit and catch him red-handed. Rather than returning yet again to Medicine Hat, why not go up the Alaska Highway all the way to Anchorage, and from there take the ferry to Nikolski?

Sarah evasively dismissed the idea. When pressed to explain why, she claimed that Jonas had already left Nikolski. Sometimes she went so far as to specify that he had shipped out in the direction of Vladivostok or had flown off to Fairbanks. Usually, however, she said nothing and turned up the radio, pretending not to hear him.

Noah, who was not lacking in insight, suspected this was a bad case of cold feet—a chronic inability to go near the ocean. He was able to confirm his diagnosis through expert interrogation.

Had she ever been to Vancouver?

Pout of indifference.

Had she ever happened to leave the middle of the country?

She had never seen the point.

Didn't she feel like seeing what there was on the far side of the Rockies?

Sarah's uninspired response was that it made no sense to go see for themselves, since they had several road maps allowing them to answer that question, which was of no interest anyway. Noah, who had long ago exhausted the possibilities of the glove compartment, decided to put the question directly:

"You've never had the urge to see the Pacific Ocean?"

Sarah was content to answer, no, she had never really wanted to whiff seagull droppings or rotting seaweed. The reply, a clever blend of contempt and indifference, betrayed a poorly disguised tremor of panic.

Noah shook his head. In his miniature inner atlas he crossed out Nikolski.

Time rolled on to *Grampa*'s oceanic rhythm. Nothing seemed to have changed, other than the distribution of rust on the sides of the 1966 Bonneville. Sarah piloted, Noah grew and the trailer appeared to be forever in the grips of a circular curse. It was sighted in July near Lake of the Woods, on the Ontario border; on Christmas Eve it was caught unawares in southern

Alberta, in the empty parking lot of a People's store; in March it showed up at the far northern edge of Lake Winnipegosis, trapped by a blizzard at a truck stop; in May it was criss-crossing southern Saskatchewan. Come July, it could be seen once again at Lake of the Woods, having returned to its point of departure with the migratory punctuality of a sperm whale.

Noah had made friends with no one—an unpleasant but necessary decision. When their trailer whisked past a schoolyard he contemplated the throng of potential companions. There were hundreds of them on the other side of the chain-link fence, playing basketball, complaining about their teachers, clustering in circles to puff on a cigarette. Some of them gazed yearningly at the road. The old silvery trailer exerted on them a strange magnetic force, like a Mongol horde galloping across the suburbs of a large city. With their fingers threaded through the grid, the captives envied the nomads.

Noah considered the possibility of throwing himself out the window.

He did not share in the Glorious North American Motoring Myth. To his mind, the road was nothing but a narrow nowhere, bounded on the starboard and port sides by the real world, a fascinating, inaccessible, unimaginable place. Most of all, the road bore no relation to Adventure, Freedom or the Absence of Algebra Homework.

Every fall, Sarah bought the appropriate school-books, and he would lock himself in the trailer to study zealously, in the belief that algebra and grammar represented his only hope of one day joining the real world.

Twelve years had gone by since the postcard from Nikolski. Noah was now eighteen—the time had come to leave the trailer. All he was waiting for to set his escape plan in motion were the results of his Manitoba Department of Education exams. Once he had secured his grade twelve diploma, he would be off to university.

He was far less concerned with choosing his field of study than with the location of the university itself. It was out of the question for him to take up residence in Winnipeg or Saskatoon; Noah wanted to climb out of the glove compartment and vault over the horizon. But which horizon exactly?

South? The United States did not interest him.

North? Not a viable option so long as there were no plans to open a Central University of Baffin Island.

West? The West was riddled with holes, as transparent and greasy as the road maps in the glove compartment. West was his father, that far-off and mysterious man who lived with an Aleutian tribe on an island lost in the Bering Sea, who ate raw salmon and heated his yurt with dried sheep turds—not the most edifying father figure to look up to.

So Noah would go east.

He wrote on the sly to a Montreal university. The registration papers arrived a week later at Armada General Delivery.

Noah was afraid to reveal his plan to his mother. He anticipated a tirade against Montreal, the port city, gateway to the St. Lawrence Seaway, frenzied metropolis— neither more nor less than a man-eating leviathan. What took place was nothing like that. Puckering her lips with indifference, Sarah watched him rip open the envelope.

"An *island*," was all she bothered to mumble.

Rather than wasting his energy on futile rebuttals, Noah withdrew to the trailer to study the contents of the envelope, especially the program directory, a thick atlas of the various trajectories that now offered themselves to him. He began by looking for the Diploma in Applied Nomadology or the B.A. in International Roaming, the only disciplines for which he felt he had some talent, but there was no mention of any such degrees. He would have to make do with whatever other options were available.

Noah set about reading the directory from cover to cover, leaving nothing out, from Abstruse Sciences to Zenology, taking in Abyssometrics, Opinion Machining and Studies in Applied Mercantilism along the way. Overcome in short order by this soporific reading material, he keeled over with his face in the directory.

He resurfaced an hour later, feeling nauseous. He looked about, hoping to recognize his surroundings.

The kettle reflected a distorted image of his face. In the very centre of his forehead the cheap ink had stamped a puzzling word: *Archaeology*.

Noah shrugged his shoulders, and surmised that there was no denying the force of destiny.

When Sarah finally emerges from her sleeping bag, the fog has lifted and Noah has prepared the breakfast table. They eat in silence, amid the herbicidal fumes rising from the drainage ditch. Noah takes a half-hearted bite out of his toast with honey and then leaves it practically untouched. Sarah is content with two scalding cups of tea.

Breakfast ends abruptly. Sarah scoops up the jar of honey and the teapot and folds down the table as though she feels a sudden sense of urgency.

While she organizes the departure, Noah checks his pack one last time; it contains the strict minimum, each item carefully considered. From the kitchen table, the Chipewyan ancestors follow the tiniest gesture with their usual incomprehension.

Then, sitting on his bunk, Noah slowly scans the interior of the trailer in the hope of finding a detail that by some miracle may have escaped his attention over the last eighteen years. He finds nothing, and ends his stock-taking with a sigh.

He tightens the straps on his pack, slings it over his shoulder and steps out of the trailer.

Sarah is already sitting in the car, hands on the steering wheel, eyes on the road, in an attitude of both impatience and denial. Noah opens the other door and begins to get in, one foot in the car, the other on solid ground. He holds this position for several minutes without speaking, his gaze turned westward.

"Should I drop you off at the Trans-Canada?" Sarah finally asks.

Squinting, Noah contemplates tiny Route 627. Not much traffic in these parts, but what does it matter? There's no hurry. Sarah reluctantly starts up *Grampa*'s engine. She listens to the low rumbling of the V-8, on the alert for any suspicious noises, while Noah searches for a memorable phrase to close this chapter of his life.

Suddenly, Sarah reaches over to the glove compartment, punches it open and grabs the Book with No Face.

"Don't forget this."

Noah wavers for a moment, partially opens his pack and squeezes the old book between two sweaters. The binding is as brittle as bone and the old map of the Caribbean comes loose, orphaned in his hands.

After this, everything happens very quickly: Sarah, without a word, hugs him with all her strength, and then boots him out of the car. Before he has time to add another word, she puts the car in gear and tears off in a clatter of gravel, with the passenger door still open.

A minute later Noah finds himself alone on the side of the road, backpack agape, an old map of the Caribbean in his hand and a ball of asphalt in his stomach. He breathes deeply, folds the map and slips it into his shirt pocket. Then he adjusts his backpack and starts walking east, eyes squinting directly into the sun, which is still suspended on the horizon.

A little farther along, three crows are pecking at the carcass of an animal. Noah shoos away the birds, which caw indignantly as they take flight, only to perch on the far side of the road.

Beached on the gravel, eyes turned skyward, a large sturgeon, a casualty of the road, watches the clouds sail by.

Tête-à-la-Baleine

JOYCE OPENS ONE EYE. The alarm clock says a quarter to five. She dresses in silence, without turning on the light. She pulls her duffel bag from under the bed, hoists it onto her shoulder and tiptoes out of the room. Her uncle's snoring upstairs blends with the purring of the refrigerator.

Outside, a cloud of mist rises from her mouth. To the west, the moon has just gone down and the faint winkling of the last stars can just be made out. Joyce sets out at a brisk pace and avoids looking at the neighbours' houses.

A few minutes later, she reaches the high school.

She glances blankly at the schoolyard —orange gravel under the mercury arc lamp—and realizes she feels nothing anymore, neither disgust or contempt. She is surprised at how quickly the past and forgetting have fallen into step behind her. Twelve hours ago she was still a prisoner of this enclosure, yet now the place seems completely foreign to her. Not even the despicable Frost fence bothers her now. Of course, the appearance of a fence changes considerably depending on which side of it you are standing. And on this side, the latticework is reminiscent only of the harmless grid of a geographic map.

She lengthens her stride.

When she was six years old, Joyce used to slip furtively into her father's office. She would close the door without a sound, weave her way among the piles of Fisheries and Oceans Department publications, the boxes full of government forms, the catalogues of buoys, and withdraw from the cabinet some long rolls of paper. She would remove the elastic bands and unfurl on the floor dozens of nautical charts of every scale and colour, most of them covered with notes, calculations and hastily delineated fishing zones.

Joyce developed a particular preference for chart 274-B, an immense projection on a scale of 1:100,000 of the coastline of the Lower North Shore with, at its very centre, the tiny village of Tête-à-la-Baleine. She had unrolled this chart so many times that its edges had turned a parchment colour. When examined against the light, the blue of the sea revealed an intricate archipelago of greasy finger marks interspersed with currents, depth markings, buoys, seamarks, lighthouses and channels.

In one corner of the chart, near the legend, was this printed warning:

THE READINGS TAKEN IN THE COASTAL ZONES BETWEEN SEPT-ÎLES AND BLANC-SABLON DO NOT MEET MODERN STANDARDS. UNMAPPED ROCKS AND SHALLOWS MAY EXIST IN THIS AREA. CAUTION MUST BE EXERCISED WHEN NAVIGATING THESE WATERS.

And, indeed, the local topography displayed an astonishing number of islands, islets, reefs, peninsulas, mirages, wrecks and buoys, as well as innumerable rocks that surfaced here and there at low tide.

While the nautical charts of the region showed an abundance of islands, there was at the same time a glaring lack of roads. This might have been put down to an omission intrinsic to nautical charts, whose primary function is to facilitate navigation, but the reason was much less obscure; the maps showed no roads quite simply because there were none. The 138 stopped at Havre-St-Pierre and resurfaced briefly at Pointe-aux-Morts. The stretch between those two points—350 nautical miles strewn with the aforementioned shallows—was serviced by ship and airplane.

This dearth of roads produced two significant effects.

The first was that the people of Tête-à-la-Baleine travelled very little. They were content to practise a seasonal variety of nomadism known as transhumance, which involved spending the summer on Providence Island, a few miles from the coast. This collective migration had in times past made it possible to move

closer to the cod shoals during the fishing season. Which raised a question: Now that the cod fishers moored their boats at the Tête-à-la-Baleine municipal wharf, why had no one thought of establishing a summer village of their own on another island farther out, somewhere beyond Providence? After all, there were plenty of islands nearby.

The second effect—no doubt the most important—was that Joyce, absorbed in her father's nautical charts, did not set foot outside her village before the age of twelve.

Joyce's mother had died a week after giving birth, reportedly because the head of a capelin had got trapped in her bronchial tube. The details of the story were subject to minor variations. At times it was said to have been a cod vertebra in the lungs, or a herring bone in the windpipe—but one thing was beyond dispute: she had been a victim of the sea.

As Joyce's father had never wanted to remarry, she remained an orphan and an only child, captain and commander under God, in other words, in charge of preparing the meals, cleaning the house and doing her homework by herself, all of which she performed as a matter of course by the time she was six. Cooking meant boiling or frying the incidental catches her father would bring home. As for the housekeeping, Joyce botched this job shamelessly. Her father looked with forbearance on the abiding mess.

But the most gruelling of all these chores was putting up with her father's family, an assortment of inquisitorial aunts, rowdy cousins and boisterous uncles who were apt to drop in at the slightest opportunity. Joyce's father, a big-hearted man, could not bring himself to turn out his brothers and brothers-in-law; they entered the house as if it were theirs, invited themselves for dinner, railed loudly against the cod quotas and the offshore inspectors, discussed the latest Japanese dietary trends and stayed to watch *Hockey Night in Canada*. (They were avid fans of Guy Lafleur.)

Joyce had long understood that the house provided her uncles with a neutral harbour, far from their spouses' recriminations, at least until one of the wives sallied out to hustle her stray back home, tugging him by the ear or some other bodily protuberance. Actually, this was just about the only reason Joyce's aunts ever ventured over, which did not prevent them from wagging their heads as they scanned the cluttered dwelling.

The raucous bunch of cousins made up the most problematical subgroup. They rained down like an infestation of grasshoppers, pulled Joyce's hair—which from then on she decided to wear short—tripped her up and never missed a chance to have some fun at her expense. They took advantage of her father's absence to raid the fridge, snatching beer and smoked herring which they would pick apart in front of the television. In order to drive back this wild, not fully housebroken horde, Joyce defended herself with forks and frying pans.

To offset her father's invasive family, Joyce relied on the invisible, absent family of her mother, now whittled down to a single member: Grandfather Doucet.

Lyzandre Doucet lived alone in a ramshackle house erected on the shore a few kilometres from the village. He was rarely seen outside his home, and no one ever paid him a visit.

Joyce loved everything about her grandfather: his wrinkled hands, the bandana over his left eye, the vile, port-flavoured cigarillos that he smoked all day long and, above all, the thousand amazing stories that he would relate to her endlessly. Every afternoon, after school, she would run to see him. Sitting in the kitchen, he would drink a scalding blend that left rust-coloured rings in his cups and a bitter taste in the throat, that her grandfather called tea.

It was in this kitchen that Lyzandre Doucet revealed to his granddaughter the family's great secret.

Appearances notwithstanding, he assured her, Joyce was the last descendant of a long line of pirates going back all the way to Alonzo and Herménégilde Doucette, also known—depending on the circumstances, the location and the subtleties of the prevailing grammar—as Doucet, Doucett, Douchette, Douchet, Douchez, Douçoit, Duchette, Ducette, Dowcette, Dusett, Ducit or Dousette.

Born in the harbour of Annapolis Royal in the latter half of the seventeenth century, the two coastal brothers enjoyed a brief but intense career as buccaneers. They sacked the towns of New England, rammed and seized several British vessels and ousted overly acquisitive competitors. They even carried out a risky incursion into Boston harbour in the spring of 1702. The business continued until the day Alonzo died of a common case of indigestion. Herménégilde then retired, thanks to the ample booty the two brothers had stashed away in the fogbound coves of Nova Scotia.

The Doucet family's calling as corsairs would have surely faded into the quiet mists of retirement had it not been for the signing in 1713 of the Treaty of Utrecht.

By ceding Acadia to the English, Louis XIV plunged all the settlers into a delicate situation, especially the Doucet family, whose New England raids had not been forgotten. Sensing the coming storm, Herménégilde's children anticipated the deportation and spread out in all directions, from the Baie des Chaleurs to the Gulf of Mexico.

The wandering and the political uncertainty put piracy back on the agenda.

From north to south there appeared swarms of little buccaneers, like Armand Doucet, Euphédime Doucette,

Ezéchias Doucett, Bonaventure Douchet and a number of other variably spelled Doucets whose names have hardly been retained by history. Since one pirate always attracts other pirates, many buccaneers joined the Doucet family: Captain Samuel Hall of Nova Scotia, the Newfoundlander Turk Kelly, as well as Louis-Olivier Gamache, the illustrious freebooter of Ellis Bay. Joyce's grandfather even claimed that Jean Lafitte, the legendary Louisiana pirate, was a distant cousin of sorts.

Joyce had never heard of Jean Lafitte, but she was perfectly willing to be impressed.

A century later, Joyce's great-great-grandfather and his two eldest sons built the legendary Doucet house near Tête-à-la-Baleine. Hastily assembled out of driftwood, it swayed in the nor'easter with foreboding creaks, leaning seaward like a huge marine mammal suffering vain attempts to keep it ashore. At every equinox, the whole village would place bets on the odds that the frame would finally give up and go out with the tide, but the years passed (Grandfather Doucet would declare, while pounding the nearest post with his fist) and the old building was still standing.

That house was where every Doucet of Tête-à-la-Baleine had been born and had lived: grandfather and grandmother, great-uncles and great-aunts, cousins both male and female, brothers-in-law and mangy dogs. This branch of the family had stopped practising piracy without, however, having made a profession of fishing. The absence of any precise role had gone a long way to cutting them off from the rest of the population.

In any case, the Doucets lived too far from the village not to be suspect. The town braggarts claimed to visit the rickety house to tumble their girls or to get rum, for, though Grandfather Lyzandre had never rammed and boarded any ship whatsoever, he had done his share of smuggling during Prohibition. No more was needed for the secluded house to be branded a brothel, a dive and a den of eternal damnation.

Weary of the contempt and the gossip, several members of the family considered leaving the village. The exodus began in June 1960 with the departure of Lyzandre's youngest son, Jonas Doucet.

This celebrated uncle, hardly fourteen years of age, had gone upriver to Montreal and signed on with a freighter bound for Madagascar, never to be seen again. His family would occasionally receive illegible postcards dispatched from every port in the world, which Grandfather Lyzandre thumbtacked on the walls of the house. In the depths of winter, when the nor'easter swept across the strand, the colourful stamps from Sumatra or Havana spiced up the Doucets' daily lives and made them homesick in their very own kitchen.

Uncle Jonas's leaving touched off a devastating wave of emigration among the clan. Within a decade, all the Doucets had vanished from Tête-à-la-Baleine. The elders were dead, the young ones had gone away, and soon all that remained were ghosts, old rumours and a wobbly house on the shore with a one-eyed grandfather inside it.

Joyce was thus the last of the Doucets in the village. A true descendant of her forebears, she had developed a solitary personality that lent her an air of precocious and troubling maturity. She always seemed distracted, immersed in her thoughts.

What's more, she suffered from claustrophobia, a natural condition, no doubt, for someone born into a family that was scattered far and wide across North America. She suffocated in tight spaces—the kitchen, the school, the village, her father's family—and nothing brought her more relief than to lose herself in her Grandfather Lyzandre's pirate stories, his bitter tea, and the shaky house where she would once again become the great-great-granddaughter of Herménégilde Doucette. Each night she would demand a story about a different pirate. There in that smoky kitchen, all the Doucets of the seven seas filed past, along with the likes of Samuel Bellamy, Edward Teach, Francis Drake, François L'Ollonais, Benjamin Hornigold, Stede Bonnet and William Kidd.

Joyce wanted to believe these buccaneers had once haunted the environs of Tête-à-la-Baleine, but Grandfather Lyzandre quickly set her straight: these migratory birds preferred the tropical climes. Indeed, most of them had taken up residence under the sun, in the mythical haven of Providence Island.

Joyce was perplexed by this place name; she spent
every summer on Providence Island and had never
noticed anything like a pirate's haven, nothing but old
shingled houses peopled with noisy uncles and cousins.

Lyzandre Doucet explained that there was another
island called Providence, located to the north of
Hispaniola Island, in the Caribbean. Actually, it was
situated in the middle of the Bahamas, but when it came
to accuracy one could not ask too much of Grandfather
Lyzandre, who had patched together his erudition from
old almanacs and commercial calendars.

Be that as it may, the pirates had turned this island
into an impregnable refuge where they feared no one.
They occupied a harbour with two openings, easy to
defend and too shallow for the hulking navy vessels.
No god or master held sway on Providence Island,
which from Joyce's point of view meant no uncles or
cousins, and therefore proved beyond the shadow of a
doubt that this was an entirely different island.

Little by little, the ambition of carrying on the family tradition seeped into her mind. It seemed inappro-
priate to her that the great-great-granddaughter of
Herménégilde Doucette should devote her days to
gutting cod and doing science homework. She was
destined for a pirate's life, shiver me timbers!

This brand new vocation was, however, hampered
by the lack of a role model; the Doucet family album
included not a single freebooting woman, not one nasty,

shaft-wielding matriarch whose skirts might have smelled of gunpowder and Jamaican rum. Not even a two-bit piggy-bank thief. Even Grandfather Lyzandre, with all his encyclopedic knowledge, was unable to recall any piratesses. Piracy was strictly a male affair. Joyce saw this as a grave injustice; why couldn't girls plunder, live dangerously, bury treasure, mock the law and the gallows?

So there she stayed, prisoner of a family without fame, a village without roads, a gender without options, a time without hope. Standing on the shore of Providence Island, gripping her binoculars, she watched the freighters sail through the channel. Their cargo was no longer the gold and silver of the East Indies, but wheat, crude oil, and endless rolls of paper on their way to New York, where they would serve to print thousands of kilometres of bad news.

If Herménégilde Doucette had been around, he would have died of neurasthenia within forty-eight hours.

Tête-à-la-Baleine had only an elementary school, so every September about fifteen teenagers went off to the high schools of Havre-St-Pierre, Sept-Îles or Blanc-Sablon. Their younger siblings, left behind, anxiously and impatiently contemplated the future.

That morning, a boy had just aroused a wave of admiration when he declared he would fly a helicopter, like his uncle Jacques. Another upped the ante by announcing that he would become the chief engineer on the icebreaker *Des Groseilliers*. A third would be a something-vaguely-mechanical-engineer of bridges and motors—like, you know . . . an engineer!

Joyce rarely took part in the discussions. No ques- 55
tions were ever put to this odd little cousin, who, truth to tell, went for the most part unnoticed. That morning, however, moved by a sudden surge of enthusiasm, she was careless enough to open her mouth:

"I'm going to be a pirate!"

Her words were greeted with dumbfounded silence. They all turned toward Joyce, who met their gazes without flinching. She often provoked this sort of astonishment, due, on one hand, to the discrepancy between her slight appearance and her self-assurance, and on the other hand, to her propensity for uttering ideas so bizarre, so out of touch with reality, that one wondered where on earth she might come from. At any rate, surely not from Tête-à-la-Baleine.

One of her cousins, still brooding over some whacks he'd received from a frying pan, did not miss the chance to call her a bearded lady. Another cousin objected that she was too scrawny to be a pirate.

"To be a pirate, you mainly have to be a guy," her eldest cousin ruled authoritatively. "That's why your mother abandoned you. She wanted a boy."

"My mother is dead!" Joyce snarled, grabbing her cousin by the collar.

"Your mother's not dead. She ran away! She's living in New York."

"No, Toronto!" another cousin chimed in.

"Vancouver!"

"Chicago!"

Bombarded on all sides, Joyce wavered. At this point, they were told recess was over, and the group moved toward the door. After a moment of hesitation, she swerved away in the opposite direction. Feeling they might have said too much, the boys watched her head toward the cemetery.

"Anyway," one of them muttered, "pirates don't exist anymore."

Joyce had never gone to see her mother's grave.

The choking on the head of a capelin seemed to her an indisputable fact. All the same, though, she preferred not to talk about it. That spectacular asphyxiation was part of the family mythology, made up of distinguished lives and exotic fatalities. What good was a flesh-and-blood mother, aside from dispensing household chores and admonishments? Joyce preferred an invisible, legendary mother, whose image melded with those of Herménégilde Doucette, Uncle Jonas's postcards and Providence Island.

She went around the cemetery reading every epitaph.

She confirmed what her grandfather had told her: a number of Doucets had been buried there, most of them before 1970. But she found not a single tombstone bearing her mother's given name. This absence was not a good omen.

On leaving the graveyard, she veered off toward the strand.

When she entered the shaky house, Lyzandre Doucet had just placed a steaming pot of tea on the table, as if he had been expecting his granddaughter. That day, however, she had no wish to discuss distant ancestors or seventeenth-century buccaneers; she demanded to know the truth about her mother.

Lyzandre Doucet listened patiently to his granddaughter but declined to answer her many questions. He was familiar with her fiery personality and was afraid that, on learning the truth, she would feel responsible for events beyond her grasp. Some children are prone to bearing the weight of the world on their shoulders.

"But Grampa," she insisted, "how long am I going to be able to stand up to my cousins without even a gravestone to point to?"

After half an hour of this torment, Lyzandre Doucet finally confessed that the capelin-head story was a smokescreen for a scandal that no one had ever dared reveal to her: her mother had acted just like the rest of the Doucet family. She had gone away a few months after Joyce was born, with no warning or proper explanation. She had boarded a westbound ship, but no one was aware of her exact destination. Some said it was Montreal, or even the United States.

Joyce drank her tea without saying a word. This disclosure muddled the situation a great deal. How could she be certain of what had really happened? There was no point in questioning those around her. The answer was no longer to be found in Tête-à-la-Baleine.

Frowning, Joyce mulled over the annoying absence of roads on her father's nautical charts.

Five years later, Grandfather Lyzandre, the last Doucet of Tête-à-la-Baleine, passed away, carried off by a fit of coughing. It would be the second (and last) time Joyce paid a visit to the village cemetery.

She did not seem to be greatly affected by Lyzandre's death, and continued to go to the house by the shore. Each afternoon she settled herself by the table—at the exact spot where she had found her grandfather's body calmly seated before his teapot—and looked at Uncle Jonas's postcards tacked up on the kitchen walls. No one had had the nerve to disturb the contents of the house; it was as though all of its inhabitants had been cut down by the plague. While sifting through the jumble of family objects, Joyce salvaged her own inheritance: an antique sailor's duffel bag that had no doubt belonged to her grandfather's grandfather.

Soon afterwards, Joyce's uncles boarded up the doors and windows with old planks of wood.

The house survived Lyzandre Doucet by only a few weeks. Its aging skeleton, afflicted by terminal osteoporosis, leaned farther and farther seaward. It seemed to just barely hang on to the shoreline. The great September tides gave the *coup de grâce* to its fragile footing, and it went adrift one Saturday morning. It floated for a while, and then the waves tore it apart and scattered the debris.

Uncle Jonas's postcards, misshapen and covered with purplish jellyfish, were all that came back with the tide.

Joyce heard about the wreckage only three months later. The whole village was settling the bets that had been collecting for decades at the old house's expense, but by then Lyzandre's granddaughter was already in Sept-Îles, completely taken up with her arrival at high school.

She had long looked forward to this chance to be rid of her uncles, aunts and cousins, and had not taken her father's benevolence into account. One phone call had been enough for him to arrange her accommodations, so that, stepping out from a little-known corner of her kinfolk, an uncle and aunt were there, waiting for Joyce on the pier at Havre-St-Pierre.

The intrusion of these distant relations was like a bolt from the blue. Was this family of hers inexhaustible? Joyce wondered, raising her arms up to the sky. Would she have to escape to Vladivostok in order to elude the clutches of her family tree?

Leaning over the handrail of the Nordik Express, she scanned the small crowd huddled in the pouring rain. She had never met these two new personae and did not have so much as a photograph to identify them. She finally spotted a stout individual wrapped in a green poncho, unfazed by the storm and displaying a wilted cardboard sign where one could make out the word *Joice*. Beside him, a small lady in a yellow raincoat was holding in one hand her umbrella and in the other a Tupperware container full of maple fudge.

Joyce estimated that she could easily slip by them and disappear without being noticed. She looked at the sky. The remnants of Hurricane Paloma, which had travelled up from the Bahamas, had just reached the north coast of the St. Lawrence. The rain and squalls would last for another two days.

"Bad weather for running away," Joyce reasoned as she went down the gangway.

They tossed Grandfather Doucet's old blue duffel into the back of the orange Suburban and set off toward Sept-Îles.

As she chewed on a piece of maple fudge, Joyce gave perfunctory answers to her new aunt's questions. (Yes, she'd had a good trip. Yes, she was eager to begin high school. Yes, her father was fine, and by the way sent his regards.)

What she was really thinking about, however, was just one thing: Route 138. Hypnotized, she looked at the headlights reflecting on the wet asphalt. At last she was leaving her father's nautical charts and journeying into an unmapped world, teeming no doubt with unknown perils, but where every road she might wish to take lay open to her. Later she would understand that this liberty was in fact limited to the 138, but for now she watched with fascination as the little villages slipped past: Rivière-à-la-Chaloupe, Rivière-aux-Graines, Manitou, Rivière-Pigou, Matamec and the Maliotenam reservation.

If she had been the one holding the wheel of the orange Suburban, she would have continued on to Tadoussac, Pointe-au-Pic, Quebec, all the way to Montreal, where the 138 turned into Sherbrooke Street and plunged into the mysteries of the city's core.

But it was her uncle's sweaty hands that held the steering wheel, so they stopped in Sept-Îles.

Five years passed.

Fifty thousand school days.

Two million hours of Cramer's Rule, of compound-complex sentences with appositive subordinate clauses, of the Treaty of Utrecht, of the atomic mass of potassium nitrate, of anticlinal curves, of constant acceleration in a vacuum, of gross domestic products.

Resolutely locked inside her deep-sea diver's suit, Joyce waited for the stopover to be over.

When she turned seventeen, she was told she must choose the trade she would ply for the rest of her days. This, at any rate, was the opinion of her high school career counsellor, Mr. Barrier. As earnest as a recruiting officer, he received the students one after another in his beige office. Height, weight, physical condition, psychological profile, attitudes, aptitudes—the students trooped in and out, the counsellor counselled.

Joyce's case was tricky. For all her limited social skills, her rejection of authority and her impertinence, she still managed to chalk up impeccable grades in every subject. And this excellence prevented her from being shunted aside. Mr. Barrier questioned her testily. What contribution did she think she could make to society? Sooner or later, you had to choose!

Joyce responded with an ambiguous pout. Her five years in Sept-Îles had not supplied her with any certainties. She was aware of only two passions: mathematics and cutting class. Now, it did not take a career counsellor to realize that the prospects held out by these two disciplines were less than promising. What could be in store for a homeless mathematician or a landless surveyor?

Weary of this tedious tête-à-tête, Joyce finally announced that she would like to be a cartographer. Mr. Barrier raised an astonished eyebrow but did not hazard any comments. A choice was a choice, and he would at last be able to close Joyce Kenty's troublesome employment file.

The recess bell rang just as she was leaving Mr. Barrier's office. Ten minutes of freedom before Mr. Turbing's computer science course. Joyce decided to get a breath of air.

It was a misty Thursday morning with no sky or horizon. Every step she took made a sucking noise on the ground, and an imperceptible breeze carried the scent of the sea up to the high school. Joyce walked across the yard to survey the outside world through the mesh in the chain-link fence. She looked at her watch. Only six minutes of freedom left.

She sighed.

In her view, Mr. Turbing's classes were part of a vast obscurantist conspiracy. Under his sway, the creative potential of the computer lab was reduced to that of an assembly line. His course was entirely based on Logo, a computer language that involved moving a metaphorical turtle across the monitor of a Commodore 64.

Joyce despised Logo, assembly lines and the authoritarian incompetence of Mr. Turbing.

When the bell signalled the end of recess, Joyce scrambled up the Frost fence, jumped down on the other side and headed off, while three youths sharing a spliff behind the garbage bin looked on indifferently.

Of course, it would have been simpler to leave by the main door, but why bother to swim against the tide if you're not going to do it in style?

Most of the truckers coming through Sept-Îles refuelled with diesel and caffeine at a restaurant called Chez Clément on Laure Boulevard.

Laure Boulevard was actually Route 138, and all traffic on the Lower North Shore necessarily transited through there. At its western end there was nothing special about the boulevard, but if you came in from the east, after two hundred kilometres of peat bog and scattered spruce, there was always something dazzling about the string of Dunkin Donuts, Kentucky Fried Chicken, McDonald's and the like. Overwhelmed by the glitter, motorists would not even notice Chez Clément. For the truckers, on the other hand, this was a vital oasis, one they looked forward to for hundreds of kilometres.

That morning, there were only two trucks in the huge parking lot. Joyce pushed open the restaurant door and savoured the unique atmosphere of the place: imitation wood counters, orange vinyl seats, plastic ferns, a bar section with muted lighting, and the local radio station providing background music. Two veteran truckers sat at the counter swapping the morning's gossip. Accustomed to talking over the VHF radio, they seemed careful not to interrupt each other, and inserted a brief silence between each of their replies.

Joyce installed herself within earshot of the truckers (something about a big Chrysler wedged into a guardrail) as Francine, with a knowing smile, brought her her usual black coffee and morning newspaper.

Joyce gave her a wink and took a sip of coffee.

The main front-page story was the dismantling of the Iron Curtain between Austria and Hungary. No photograph accompanied the article, so Joyce, unaided, had to picture thousands of GDR residents jostling at the border. There was also a piece about a pileup on Highway 40, and another about John Turner's resignation.

A few pages on, there was a report on the latest reduction of cod quotas. Joyce's uncles would likely be fuming for weeks. She felt a pang of joy at the thought of not having to cook for them anymore.

Then, squeezed between two ads for long-distance services at the bottom of page 54, an item suddenly caught her attention:

FBI ARRESTS TOP-RANKING PIRATE

Chicago—After months of investigation, the FBI has apprehended the leader of a major pirate gang.

The FBI yesterday arrested Leslie Lynn Doucette, a 35-year-old woman who headed the largest ring of pirates ever to be dismantled in the United States.

Doucette, who also went by the alias Kyrie, is accused of pirating computer voice mail for the purpose of planting "information lines" in the messages. It is believed these information lines allowed over 150 accomplices to exchange credit card numbers and long-distance calling card numbers. The FBI seized several hundred card numbers as well as the authorization codes of numerous corporate telephone systems. The total worth of this fraud scheme is estimated at 1.5 million USD. Doucette, a Canadian citizen, went into hiding in the U.S. in 1987 after being sentenced for similar offences perpetrated on Canadian soil. She had been living in Chicago for a number of years with her two children.

The cup of coffee stayed suspended in front of Joyce's mouth. Around her, the universe spun in slow motion. Sounds came to her in strangely distorted fragments. Time had stopped. Nothing else in the world mattered but the forty-line epiphany at the bottom of page 54.

Joyce finally came around and looked at her watch. Time was once again on the march, and in fact seemed to have sped up considerably. The two truckers paid for their coffee, dropped their tip money on the imitation wood with a clatter and went out to continue their runs, one to Havre-St-Pierre and the other to Montreal.

Joyce carefully tore out the news item, slipped it into her shirt pocket and made her way back to the high school.

It is 5:40 a.m. and still dark when Joyce arrives at Clément's restaurant the next day.

The air is saturated with various oils—unleaded, diesel, bacon grease—and the gas pumps seem to vibrate under the fluorescent lights. In the west, the last stars have gone out.

67

A dozen trucks are parked in the half-light, engines idling, running lights turned on low. A tranquil scene. Some drivers are still asleep in their cabs, others are drinking their first cup of coffee at the restaurant counter. One of them has lifted the hood of his truck and is checking the oil, a flashlight clenched between his teeth.

Without hesitating, Joyce walks toward the truck. When the driver sees her approaching, he turns the beam of his flashlight on her face.

"What do you want?" he growls.

Not exactly encouraging. Joyce has prudently taken a few steps back and, for a moment, considers turning around, going back to her bed—maybe the sheets are still warm—and dropping the whole thing.

She is about to beat a retreat when a detail brings her up short: at a certain angle, the trucker's head—gaunt face, goatee, severely receding hairline—reminds her of someone. But who? Her memories flip by like a library card catalogue. Twentieth century. Political figure. Russia. Revolution. Goatee.

With unreal precision, Joyce remembers in a flash where she saw this face for the first time: on one of Uncle Jonas's postcards!

The card had been pinned up for years in the Doucets' kitchen, right beside the King Cole calendar. It had been posted from the U.S.S.R. in November 1964, but little else was known about it, for the only legible words were those of the postmark: Ленинград—Leningrad—12 XI 1964. Each time she looked at this card, Joyce imagined her uncle Jonas in the middle of a snowstorm, his beard coated with frost, asking a bewildered longshoreman where the nearest mailbox might be.

On the back of the card was a scarlet stamp of Vladimir Lenin, pasted there like a tiny wanted poster offering a bounty of 16 kopecks for the head of the ferocious Bolshevik.

Struck dumb, Joyce stares at the trucker's severe features. There can be no mistake: here is Vladimir Lenin, lost in the parking lot of a truck stop in Sept-Îles at a quarter to six in the morning.

Joyce smiles at the anachronism. Then she gets serious again. If Uncle Jonas had the guts to haunt the icy docks of Leningrad when he was fourteen, who can prevent Joyce—no less a Doucet than he was—from doing as much?

She takes a deep breath and hazards a step in Vladimir Lenin's direction.

"I'm going to Montreal. Can you give me ride?"

Providence

JOYCE SITS SURROUNDED by marine mammal identification handbooks, rolled-up posters and piles of travel brochures. The young woman behind the steering wheel manoeuvres skilfully through the rush-hour traffic, while her co-pilot, fumbling with a map of Montreal from 1979, carps about the one-way streets.

The couple picked Joyce up seven hours earlier, aboard the ferry from Tadoussac. A stroke of luck, as they just happened to be on their way to Montreal to give a series of lectures on the whales of the estuary. The woman drove unhurriedly, fingers interlaced behind her head, steering with her knees, while her partner explained to Joyce the intricate breathing cycle of the great sperm whale.

In Quebec City, they insisted on treating Joyce to lunch. She then dozed off amid the stacks of flyers, and awoke when they were already in the heart of Montreal.

"End of the line!" the woman announces cheerfully. "Where would you like us to drop you off?"

"Anywhere is fine," Joyce answers with a shrug of her shoulders.

The woman smiles at her in the rear-view mirror, cuts sharply across the right lane and stops the old blue Hyundai next to a Metro station. Joyce collects her bag and, in the time it takes to slam the door shut, finds herself alone in Babylon.

She rubs her eyes and notes the name of the Metro station: Jean-Talon. It means nothing to her.

Where to begin? She looks around, spots a telephone booth. She pushes the door open and hefts the phone directory. A vague sense of anxiety washes over her. Can she have underestimated the population of Montreal? Her fingers speedily flip through the pages: Dombrowski, Dompierre, Donati . . . Doucet. No trace of her mother's name, not even a Doucet F.

The Montreal phone book is as deserted as the Tête-à-la-Baleine cemetery.

Joyce staggers out of the phone booth, her stomach in knots. Her reasons for running away no longer seem as clear as they did this morning. The sun is going down gradually at the far end of the boulevard. Soon it will be night, and she feels all at once very, very much alone.

She adjusts her bag on her shoulder and starts walking in no particular direction.

After two blocks she ends up at the Jean-Talon market. The air is cloying and laden with essences and odours, with wafts of alcohol, pollen, putrefaction and engine oil.

Joyce stops dead in her tracks. Never in her life has she seen so much garbage at once.

She is unable to turn her eyes away from the boxes of fruit compacted and tied up in juicy cubes, a mishmash of peels and cardboard. She contemplates the multicoloured layers of leaf stalks, leaves, vegetable cores, mangoes, grapes and pineapples, interspersed with fragmentary phrases: *Orange Florida Louisiana Nashville Pineapple Yams Mexico Avocado Manzanas Juicy Best of California Farm Fresh Product Category No.1 Product of USA.*

The accumulation of trash reaches its peak at the west end of the market. A garbage truck is parked there and two garbagemen are throwing cratefuls of flowers into the monster's mouth. From time to time, a gigantic steel jaw descends, chews up the mass of leaves and cardboard and unceremoniously gulps it down.

Joyce stares at the truck, completely spellbound by all this waste. She has never experienced such a sense of *abundance*.

Suddenly, her nose starts to twitch. She looks down and sees a Styrofoam bin stained with pink spots. She fans away a swarm of flies, squats down, holds up the bin and sniffs. Fish blood. The smell is so familiar to Joyce that she feels tears welling up in her eyes.

She pulls herself together and looks around. On the nearest storefront a huge salmon is leaping skyward, circled by the name of the business in red neon: *Poissonnerie Shanahan*.

She feels strangely relieved.

The door opens onto a jumble of antennae and pincers—*Miscou lobster, $10.99/lb*. Joyce admires the tank for a moment, then swings around while taking in the details: cod livers in oil, Norwegian bacalao, pickled periwinkles, garlic snails, freeze-dried shrimp, Bavarian-style marinated herring, sea horses in Cajun sauce. And under lock and key in a custom-built cabinet, several microscopic jars of bright orange caviar, as costly as uranium 237.

In the glass display counter, dozens of creatures are laid out on a bed of crushed ice. Joyce has seen most of these fish only in her father's reference books: tuna, snappers, goatfish, mullets, groupers, mussels, crabs, giant scallops and miniature hammerhead sharks.

Behind the counter two men are conversing in Spanish. The taller man steps up, wiping his hands. He looks Joyce up and down.

"Have you come about the job?" he asks with a Cuban accent.

"The job?"

"Do you have a résumé? No? No résumé? *No importa*. Any experience in a fish shop, at least?"

"A little," she says with some hesitation, thrown off by the turn of events.

"A little? What do you mean, *a little?* You've sorted sardine cans at the IGA?"

Joyce scowls. No one gets away with insulting the great-great-granddaughter of Herménégilde Doucette! She is about to fling a Miscou lobster at his face and clear out when the second man puts down his cloth and walks up to her, hands on hips.

A silence worthy of a Sergio Leone film settles on the fish store.

With a commanding gesture, he has Joyce come around to the other side of the counter, pulls out a peculiar orange fish, lays it on the cutting board and draws a knife out of its sheath.

"Can you fillet this?"

Joyce has trouble believing that ten minutes after arriving in Montreal, here she is with her hands on a fish, hemmed in between two inquisitorial Latinos. She sighs, picks up the knife and tests the blade with her thumb. After that, everything happens very quickly. She slices off the head of the goatfish, amputates its pectoral and dorsal fins, makes a precise incision along its back, locates the spine with the tip of the knife and, as deftly as a samurai, cuts the fish open from end to end. The blade slides back and forth along the vertebrae. Joyce extracts the skeleton, a slimy jade jewel which she nonchalantly chucks into the garbage can.

Fifteen seconds by the clock.

The two men inspect the fillets, nodding their heads in approval.

"¡*Vale!* Can you start tomorrow morning?"

Joyce leaves the Poissonnerie Shanahan with instructions to come back the next day at nine a.m. sharp. She crosses the street and, when she is certain no one is watching her, takes a whiff of the blood smell still clinging to the palm of her hand. With her eyes closed she can almost believe she is back in her father's kitchen in Tête-à-la-Baleine.

A streak of blue and white jolts her out of her reverie.

A police car glides ahead of her with the quiet slowness of a shark. The driver turns his head in her direction, sunglasses covering his selachian gaze. A shiver travels through Joyce from her coccyx to the nape of her neck.

The car drives off going south. Joyce lets out a sigh of relief and looks at her watch, which tells her it is getting late. A red sign in the glass door of an old building attracts her attention. *For Rent—furnish 1½—heeting and electristy incl—now vacant see janitor in basemint.*

She ventures down to the *basemint*, and wavers between the furnace room and an unmarked door. She knocks on both. The janitor, yawning, opens the unmarked door. A Kraft Dinner aroma drifts out from the apartment.

"I'm interested in the one-and-a-half," Joyce tells him.

The janitor looks straight at her without speaking, and scratches the rim of his belly button. He leans against the door jamb, revealing nearly all of his tiny apartment: floor strewn with dirty clothes, piles of pizza boxes, closet filled with three rusted sinks, messy toolbox. And a TV set playing an old episode of *Miami Vice* at maximum volume.

"Do you have a job?" he finally mumbles, noisily raking his fingers over his three-day beard.

"At the Poissonnerie Shanahan, right across the street."

He sniffs, grabs a heavy set of keys and, without a word, starts to climb the stairs ahead of Joyce.

They go up to the third floor and stop in front of apartment 34. The door is scarred with numerous gouges from a crowbar. The janitor peevishly sifts through his set of keys. He quickly loses patience and begins to try the keys one at a time. The lock finally responds, with a metallic click and the creaking of wood.

The inside looks exactly like the outside: half the cupboard handles have gone missing, a light bulb hangs out of its socket with its optic nerves exposed, some sickly lotuses are flowering around the window, the bathroom is cramped, the refrigerator was manufactured at about the same time as the first Apollo rockets, the walls are pocked with cigarette burns and, as for the carpet, its uncertain colour tends toward Soviet green.

Rounding off the picture is a suffocating stench, a blend of stale air, mould and rug disinfectant.

Joyce examines the room with a blissful smile, dazzled by the mere prospect of having her own little Providence Island.

"I'll take it," she stammers, and sets Grandfather Lyzandre's duffel bag down on the floor.

The janitor utters a growl—*One growl for yes, two growls for no*, Joyce concludes—and goes downstairs to get a blank lease form.

Now alone, she pulls out of her pocket the newspaper clipping about Leslie Lynn Doucette, smoothes it out on her thigh, and pins it to the wall with a rusty thumbtack that she has found lying around.

Political Refugees Get Priority

STE-CATHERINE STREET. Seated at an imitation marble table covered with puddles of drying coffee, Noah has just finished his first letter to Sarah. He pushes aside the clutter of glasses, unfolds his road map of Manitoba and studies the landscape with his pen in his mouth.

Sarah is in the south of the province, somewhere in this maze of villages, of roads laid out in a grid, of rivers that run in a straight line for hundreds of kilometres because nothing gets in their way. All the areas of the map look alike. Yet she can't be everywhere! Where should he send his letter? Manitou, Grande-Clairière, Baldur? After a series of sketchy calculations, Noah addresses it to General Delivery in Ninga.

At the next table, a vagrant wearing a Maple Leafs hockey tuque is talking to himself. This no longer surprises Noah, who has gotten the impression that all Montrealers talk to themselves. He licks the flap of the envelope, folds it down carefully and wipes a bead of saliva off the paper.

The next part is the most difficult: the return address.

Noah spreads the *Journal de Montréal* over the road map, opens it to the "Apartments for Rent" section and peruses the columns of cryptic abbreviations and unknown neighbourhoods. He came into town less than forty-eight hours ago and knows nothing about the local geography. Mile End, Hochelaga, Longueuil—where should he live? He finally gives up and, with his eyes shut, points arbitrarily.

When he opens his eyes his finger has landed in the middle of an intriguing ad:

> TO SHARE 4½ PETITE ITALIE NON-SMOKER
> NO PETS FREE IMMEDIATELY.
> POLITICAL REFUGEES GET PRIORITY.
> CALL POISSONNERIE SHANAHAN ASK FOR MAELO.

At the next table the monologue grows more intense, with the guy pointing a threatening index finger at an imaginary listener. Noah reads the ad over again twice and decides this is the ideal offer. He fishes a handful of change from the bottom of his pocket and goes out in search of a telephone booth.

After three rings, a young girl answers. She speaks with an edgy voice and a curious accent. Noah asks for Maelo, who comes to the phone.

"I'm calling about the four-and-a-half to share. Is it still available?"

"It's still available," Maelo affirms. "You know I give priority to political refugees?"

Stammering, Noah says, "I come from Alberta." 79

"Okay," Maelo answers, apparently satisfied. "So, how about we meet at five-thirty?"

Starry ray, rainbow smelt, sturgeon, herring, sardine, sea trout, eel, cod, hake, threebearded rockling, John Dory, mullet, red goatfish, thicklip grey mullet, Atlantic bonito, swordfish, ocean perch, Norway redfish, American plaice, lumpsucker, dab, rock sole, Atlantic saury—the apartment is teeming with fish. They swim on every wall, in the form of posters, postcards and polychrome rubber scale models.

The place is clean and tidy, but Noah notices nothing except the fish. Has he stepped into the abode of some sort of fish fiend?

"This is the first time in ten years the room is unoccupied," Maelo explains. "I've always lived with a dozen cousins. They showed up at the rate of one a month. Every night we had to figure out how to make room for everyone. We would sleep on the couch, on the floor, under the table. We would take turns sleeping."

Noah's eyes are wide open. You can have enough cousins to fill an entire apartment like this one?

"But where did they come from?"

"From San Pedro de Macorís, in the Dominican Republic. My whole family is from there. Five generations of Guzmáns in an unbroken line. My great-grandfather founded the city, and today all my cousins are leaving for New York or Montreal."

"They don't like San Pedro?"

"Oh, no, nothing like that, they adore San Pedro. But you can earn a better living here. Now my grandmother Úrsula has been left all alone in the family house. Ninety-three years old, as hard-headed as a tortoise. She's never travelled more than five kilometres from the sea. Well, this would be your room. It's not very big, but . . ."

Noah steps gingerly into the room. *Not very big?* This one room alone contains as much living space as all of the old silver trailer. He feels like a cosmonaut who has gone out for a walk around his Soyuz and discovers the void in every direction: millions of stars, infinite spaces, and pangs of nausea. He holds onto the door jamb.

"So tell me, why have you come to Montreal?"

"I'm here to study archaeology," Noah gasps, wiping the sweat from his neck.

"Archaeology? Cool! I'm going to have an intellectual for a roommate! Listen, if you want the room, it's yours. Ordinarily, I would ask 170 not including electricity, but in your case 160 will be fine."

"When can I move in?"

"Right away. Do you have a lot to move?"

"Everything is in here," Noah answers, patting the side of his backpack.

Maelo looks at the pack and smiles.

"We're dealing with a genuine refugee! I'll lend you some sheets."

The mattress is lumpy, the pillow completely flat, and the quilt is studded with starfish, but none of it should prevent a good night's sleep. As soon as the bed has been made, the apartment-sharing arrangement is finalized with the payment of the first month's rent, an outlay that reduces Noah's wealth to the square root of zero.

Here is a crucial question: How will Noah manage to fall asleep in such a huge space?

Lying amid the starfish, he can hear the air throb around his bed and the tiniest sound wave bounce and amplify on the walls. He has never had a space that belonged to him alone—except the pygmy-size bunk bed in the silvery trailer—and he doubts that he will be able to fill up these thirty cubic metres of outer space with his meagre assets: three road maps, some clothing, a pad of letter paper and an old book with no cover.

In sum, he feels unworthy of occupying this place, as if he were afraid of wasting something. But what exactly would he be wasting? Space? Cubic centimetres? Emptiness?

Can emptiness be wasted?

Scale 1:1

THE NORTHERN BLUEFIN TUNA (*Thunnus thynnus*) is an astonishing animal.

A good-sized female can lay as many as twenty-five million eggs at a time. This profusion testifies to the voraciousness of the tuna's predators. Each microscopic larva has no more than one chance in forty million of reaching the adult stage, eight years hence. The survivors grow into superb creatures—a fifteen-year-old tuna can easily measure three metres in length and weigh in at three hundred kilos. Some individuals, though rare, can weigh up to seven hundred kilos. Such specimens are called, rather perceptively, Giants.

Tunas are gregarious and tend to gather according to size: the smaller they are, the more densely populated their schools will be. Conversely, the Giants often swim alone. They are wonderful swimmers, and from one season to the next they migrate over unimaginable distances. They spend the summer beneath the Arctic Circle, and in the winter take refuge in the tropics, travelling from one hemisphere to the other as easily as a city-dweller changes neighbourhoods. Some specimens tagged in the Bahamas have later been sighted in Norway and Uruguay.

To produce a kilo of protein, a bluefin tuna must swallow 8 kilos of herring, herring that have previously consumed 70 kilos of miniature shrimp, which in turn have ingested some 200 kilos of phytoplankton. Thus, beyond outward appearances, 2.5 kilos of tuna lying on crushed ice in a fish store represents something like a half-ton of plankton—a terrifying equation that would drive away the customers if it were revealed to them by mistake.

"The golden rule of fish stores," Maelo explains, "is *never* mention the food chain to the customers. This isn't Japan."

Because, as everyone knows, the Japanese have strong stomachs and steely eyes, and they buy their tuna at auctions held right on the blood-soaked wharves. The clientele of the Poissonnerie Shanahan is, shall we say, more delicate, being by and large made up of suburbanites from Laval-des-Rapides, Chomedey or Duvernay. But one should not be fooled by the innocuous demeanour of these predators. According to some estimates, the bluefin tuna population in the Atlantic has declined by 87 per cent since 1970, a rate that matches quite closely the expansion of the suburbs over the same period.

"It can thus be deduced," Maelo concludes, "that suburban development is very much in step with the movement of the tuna shoals."

He slices a thin strip of raw tuna, slides it into his mouth and chews it with an ambivalent expression on his face. He seems torn between his respectful admiration for the Giants, and the delicate taste of their flesh—an insoluble dilemma. He shakes his head and puts down the knife. The sashimi lesson is over.

Fifteen-minute break. Joyce pours herself a cup of black, too-sweet Dominican coffee, and goes to sit in the back doorway with her feet propped up on an empty box of mussels. A sip of coffee and a thin smile. She watches the already familiar bustle of the Jean-Talon market. What seemed larger than life a few days earlier has now taken on familiar proportions, a scale of 1:1.

It has been seven days since she ran away, and Joyce is becoming accustomed to her new routine. She shows up at work exactly on time, listens dutifully to Maelo's biology lessons, smiles at the fussiest customers and makes progress with her Spanish. Her aim is to become a model employee, to blend in with the great mass of sardines in the shoal, to dissolve into the ecosystem.

The golden rule of running away: Pay attention to your camouflage.

In this regard, Joyce could take some pages out of her own mother's book. She has looked up all the possible variations of her name in the phone directory and harassed a half-dozen telephone operators, all to no avail. Did she assume a new identity and start a new life with a suburbanite? Has she gone into exile in the Bahamas? Is she still alive, even? A total mystery.

Joyce has the feeling that the last ties with her buccaneering forebears are slowly unravelling. She hangs on to the newspaper clipping about Leslie Lynn Doucette as the ultimate proof that the family vocation has not died out. And yet she knows nothing about this distant cousin. She has no idea of her plans, her buccaneering techniques, her favourite targets, her modus operandi and, especially, the fatal error that allowed the FBI to nab her.

Joyce will have to learn everything on her own. Piracy is a self-taught discipline.

Maelo appears in the doorway and announces that there will be an exciting lesson on the anatomy of the octopus (*Octopus vulgaris*). Joyce finishes her coffee and stands up.

"So tell me, Maelo, if I'm not mistaken, you come from the Dominican Republic, right?"

"You're not mistaken."

"And Miguel and Enrique, they're from Cuba, right?"

"Right."

"So why doesn't your fish store have a Spanish name?"

"Because of the Irish immigrants who used to work in the Miron quarry at the start of the century. Every

Sunday afternoon, they would play lacrosse right on this spot. They called it the Shanahan Athletic Club. Over the years, the lacrosse field became a bus station and then the Jean-Talon market. All that's left now is Shanahan Street. You see down there at the other end of the market? That's where the fish store used to be."

"And where have the Irish gone?"

"I have no idea. But the Miron quarry has been turned into a garbage dump."

San Pedro de Macorís

THERE ARE TWO SAN PEDRO DE MACORISES.

The first is located on the southeast coast of the Dominican Republic, at 18 degrees north, 69 degrees east. The second occupies the eastern side of St-Laurent Boulevard in Montreal, in a perimeter bounded to the west by Christophe-Colomb, to the north by an imaginary line running through the de Castelnau Metro station, and to the south by the Colmado Real grocery store, on St-Zotique Street.

Maelo was the founding citizen of this second San Pedro. He arrived alone in the middle of winter in 1976 and learned everything the hard way: the cold, the French language, the geography of Montreal, the bureaucracy, Radio-Canada, *pâté chinois*, unemployment and Guy Lafleur. He found this mixture hard to stomach. He soon considered calling the whole thing off and going back to his hometown, but while he was rolling some coins he was saving to buy his return ticket, a cousin, the first of many, called to announce that he had arrived at Mirabel airport.

Maelo's hopes were renewed. Reinforcements were on the way!

He had started out as a shy immigrant and became a *89* colonizer. The bonds between San Pedro de Macorís and Montreal grew stronger, woven as they were out of enthusiastic letters, chaotic telephone calls, and Western Union money transfers. Family members began to pour in. Cousins invaded the airport, euphoric and shivering. Maelo played the role of the seasoned veteran. He housed the newcomers, found them employment, gave them food and drink and then released them into the wilds. And without intending to, he became the gravitational centre of this new community. He organized fiestas and *cenas*, meetings, lunches, get-togethers in cafés. And when there was nothing on the agenda, people went to lounge at his house as if it were the public square of some invisible city.

These gatherings culminated on the night of the Dominican presidential elections of 1986, when Maelo announced the holding of a great *jututo*—a meeting that involved the whole family protesting against the candidacy of Joaquín Balaguer, drinking rum and then quarrelling over the future of the republic.

Balaguer was re-elected, the neighbours complained about the racket, and the *jututo* became a regular event. Now, on Sunday nights, Maelo gathers in the fruit of the family tree: his four brothers, three sisters, a dozen cousins, childhood friends and a few random refugees—stray Guatemalans or some Cubans just passing through. The merrymakers devour conches and shrimp, goatfish and giant mussels, kilos of rice and *habichuelas*, *guandules*, and yucca—all of it washed down with Concha y Toro, Brugal Añejo and *mamajuana*. Then they dance the *bachata* until the wee hours and remodel the world from top to bottom, with the Caribbean getting the bulk of their attention.

According to Maelo, an immigrant can be adrift, confused, shy, exhausted, exploited, unwilling to adapt, drowning in depression, wallowing in nostalgia. But he must never stoop to being an orphan.

Colmado Real

NOAH GOES INTO THE POST OFFICE, carefree, jiggling in the palm of his hand the small change he will use to buy a stamp. In the other hand he holds the envelope of miracles, adorned with his mother's name, the General Delivery address in Ninga and a return address, a reassuring fixed point in the universe.

He stops suddenly in the middle of the room, completely stunned.

The air is suffused with the aroma of the thousands of post offices scattered over the plains from Winnipeg to Calgary. Crushed paper, elastic bands, rubber stamps.

Noah falters. Right at that moment he is catapulted three thousand kilometres away, thirteen years earlier. He blinks and looks around. What if Montreal was just one more General Delivery? He thought he was stepping onto solid ground when he left his mother's trailer, but now that ground is slipping out from under him. At this point he feels nothing but rolling waves, choppy seas and dizziness.

He takes a deep breath and tries to think straight. What is a smell, after all? A pinch of molecules adrift in the atmosphere. Some vague stimuli circulating between the olfactory epithelium and the frontal lobe of the cortex. The crackle of electricity, chemical reactions, enzymes, neurotransmitters—a commonplace chain of events that nevertheless upsets the delicate balance of the neurons, disturbs the mamillary bodies and dislodges old childhood memories from the benign inertia where they have been hiding.

Noah buys a stamp, sticks it on the envelope, drops the letter down the chute and leaves the office without looking back. Altogether, seventy-five seconds without taking a breath.

He returns to his apartment downhearted, a lost look in his eyes, hands held behind his back with invisible handcuffs. Seeing him go by, Maelo feels his pulse accelerating. He recognizes that look, having seen it a thousand times on his cousins' faces—the look of homesickness. The symptoms are pretty much the same for a Dominican as they are for a native of Saskatchewan. Ultimately, humanity is not as unpredictable as it's often made out to be, and Maelo knows exactly what to do. With the firm authority of an old midwife, he intercepts his roommate.

"Noah, you have to take the bull by the horns."

"Take the bull by the horns?" Noah repeats, without actually coming out of his fog.

"The first days are the hardest, but you have to rouse yourself. First, we're going to get you a job. I would take you on at the fish store, but I've just hired a girl. Instead, you're going to go see César Sánchez."

93

César Sánchez, a taciturn Dominican forever chewing on cheap cigars, is the supreme helmsman of Colmado Real. Permanently posted in the window of his grocery store is a sign inviting applications for a bicycle delivery job. The cardboard sign is baked from the heat waves of many summers and warped by countless January frosts. Noah infers from this that Colmado Real delivery boys don't hang around long enough to draw their pension.

With an extinguished Montecristo screwed into the corner of his mouth, César Sánchez X-rays Noah with his eyes:

"Do you know the neighbourhood?" he manages to ask.

"I was born on Dante Street," Noah declares without batting an eyelash.

"You're going to do a test run for me. Prepare Mme Pichet's order and deliver it to her. *¡Dale!*"

He thrusts an old notebook into his hands. On the top page someone has scrawled a half-French, half-Spanish grocery list.

"Do you supply the bicycle?" Noah asks as he rolls up his sleeves.

"*¡Claro!*" the manager exclaims, laughing, pointing to a shiny, modified 1977 CCM parked outside the display window.

The primitive vehicle is equipped with the bare essentials: three wheels, two pedals, a basket. Noah feels himself going weak in the knees. He has never before mounted a bicycle. At the age when one usually learns the basics of bike-riding, he was sorting out old road maps while watching the schoolyards slip past.

Summoning his courage, he runs up and down the aisles collecting the items on the list. Then he checks the address written at the bottom of the list.

"Gaspé Avenue?"

He shrugs and goes out to load the bags into the delivery basket, discreetly grabbing a map of Montreal as he passes the cash register.

Meet Your New Macintosh

JOYCE IS VENTING HER ANGER on some garbage bags, which she kicks one after the other.

In the street, people are working. A tired-looking man distributes flyers, some city workers bring down a hundred-year-old maple with a chainsaw, a pizza deliveryman climbs a stairway holding a steaming box. And Joyce grumbles as she watches all of them bustling about.

Since she arrived in Montreal she has done nothing but sell fillets of sole, prepare salmon steaks and smile at the customers. Any more of this and she'll start to think she's six years old again, cooking for her uncles and doing her natural history lessons like a good little girl.

The current situation would certainly displease her fearsome ancestor, the pirate Herménégilde Doucette. "What an idea, working in a fish store," he would growl with his spent voice, "when all you need to do is go down to the harbour and get aboard a ship."

"But Grampa," Joyce would plead with her arms spread wide, "this is 1989!"

"So what difference does that make?"

How could one explain? This world is no longer like the old one. Cash registers, automatic bank machines, credit card transactions, mobile telephones. It won't be long before North America is just a series of interconnected computer networks. Those able to handle a computer will get by. The others will miss the boat.

Joyce gives a cardboard box a solid kick.

She suddenly notices some guy hurtling toward her on a delivery bike, apparently more interested in the architecture than in where he is going. He jumps the curb, brushes past the garbage bags, misses Joyce by a hair and careens back into the street. She watches this Bronze Age vehicle move away and vanish down an alley.

"What about him?" she mutters. "Is he happy to be delivering grocery orders?"

She has stopped in front of a bundle of old newspapers. The top one carries an advertisement for *This Week's Specials*. The featured item in this otherwise austere quarter-page is an IBM 286 with a 50 MHz processor, 1 meg of RAM, a 30-meg hard disk, a 1.44 floppy drive, VGA display, laser printer—all for $2,495 (plus tax).

Closing her eyes, Joyce divides the price by the minimum wage. This outrageous apparatus represents over four hundred hours of lopping off cods' heads!

She sighs and lets fly a vicious kick at the nearest garbage bag. The plastic splits open and a half-dozen floppy disks tumble out haphazardly on the sidewalk. Joyce examines one of them. Under a small, multi-coloured apple is a tantalizing invitation: *Meet Your New Macintosh*.

Joyce turns toward the heap of refuse, transfigured.

CCM

⟿

NOAH INSTANTLY FELL IN LOVE with César Sánchez's old bike.

Standing on the pedals, with a firm grip on the rim of the basket, head down, he feels as though he's sailing over the neighbourhood. The hazards of the road disappear. No more traffic, no more one-way streets, no more driving regulations. All that remain are the landmarks, stretched by speed: the Jean-Talon market, the St-Zotique church, an elderly man sitting on his bench, the statue of old Dante Alighieri, the alternating butcher shops and shoe-repair shops, a tree-lined sidewalk.

The deliveryman's job, which he initially viewed as dreary, suddenly seems to him like an ideal way to map out the neighbourhood. Riding his bike, he constructs an aerial view of the territory—squares, alleyways, walls, graffiti, schoolyards, stairways, variety stores and snack bars—and when he talks with the customers, he gathers intelligence on accents, clothing, physical traits, kitchen smells and bits of music. Added together, the two catalogues make up a complex map of the area, at once physical and cultural.

He tries to transpose his observations onto a map of Montreal, but two dimensions are not enough to contain the wealth of information. Instead he would need a mobile, a game of Mikado, a matryoshka or even a series of nested scale models: a Little Italy containing a Little Latin America, which contains a Little Asia, which in turn contains a Little Haiti, without forgetting of course a Little San Pedro de Macorís.

For the first time in his life, Noah is starting to feel at home.

Fishing for the Big One

JOYCE IS SITTING on the fire escape nursing a beer. In her lap lies a ragged Spanish handbook (retrieved from the trash bins of a language school); she is memorizing the irregular verbs of the *pretérito*. At her feet, a patched-up radio is tuned to the ten p.m. news.

There is trouble in Baie-Comeau: a handful of demonstrators are trying to stop a Soviet freighter carrying PCBs from St-Basile-le-Grand from mooring in the harbour. The toxic oil was denied entry by the port authorities in Liverpool, and now an attempt is being made to discreetly hide it away on the North Shore. The Sûreté du Québec riot squad and the citizens are battling for control of the pier, while the Soviets look on and curse.

The news report comes and goes, crackles and disappears. Between two magnetic storms, Premier Robert Bourassa discusses environmental management and the upcoming provincial election. Joyce yawns and kicks the radio off. She drains her beer and scans the immediate vicinity. All is quiet. On the opposite side of the street a cloud of phosphorescent plankton is drizzling around a lamppost.

The night is young, and the alcohol has blurred the contours of the cosmos. She decides to go fishing.

Where do old IBMs go to die? Where is the secret burial ground of TRS-80s? The charnel house of Commodore 64s? The ossuary of Texas Instruments?

These are the questions that are on Joyce's mind as she picks through the rubbish of Little Italy. So far, she has salvaged a host of useful items—a radio, a fan, a work stool, vinyl records—but as far as computers go, her only bite has been an ancient, charred Atari. And yet people must somehow get rid of their old, obsolescent computers.

Behind St-Hubert Plaza, she comes upon a colleague ransacking the bottom of a trash container. His head dives down, bobs up, dives again, while his flashlight sporadically illuminates the surrounding walls.

Joyce approaches, coughing a little to make her presence known. The man lifts his head out of the container. He looks like a mad scientist: fiftyish, round glasses, a small white beard, and a scar shaped like a Möbius strip under his left eye.

"Is the fishing good?" Joyce asks with a look of innocence.

"Not bad at all. I've located a shoal of Italian footwear."

"Anything else?"

"What are you after?"

"Computers."

"Fishing for the big one," he says, with a whistle of approval. "This isn't the right area to get a bite. The best place for computer equipment is in the business district. The Stock Exchange, IBM, Place Bonaventure . . . Get the picture?"

"Not really. I'm new to Montreal."

"Give me a second."

The man scribbles some directions on the back of a business card.

"Here. And watch out for the security guards."

She examines the card. On the front she reads, *Thomas Saint-Laurent Ph.D: Department of Anthropology.* On the back is a tiny treasure map with streets, alleys, underground parking lots and Metro stations.

Joyce smiles. The time is a quarter to midnight and she does not feel the least bit sleepy anymore.

Texas Instruments

IT IS EXTREMELY CALM at the corner of de Maison-neuve and Guy.

A few pedestrians hurry toward the Guy-Concordia Metro station, chins buried in their scarves. Away from the street, camouflaged behind a metal lattice and a row of decorative sumacs, is the service entrance to a building. The blandness of the place has been carefully thought out. There is nothing to attract one's attention except for two signs: ENTRÉE INTER-DITE / ENTRANCE FORBIDDEN and ATTENTION: CETTE ZONE EST SOUS SURVEILLANCE ÉLECTRONIQUE.

Joyce slips inside, takes a deep breath and analyzes the situation. At the very back of the parking lot, near the loading docks, are three dumpsters. She pulls on her work gloves and advances, looking in every direction. No security cameras in sight. She lifts the lid of the first container and sweeps the beam of her flashlight over its contents.

A computer keyboard is jutting out from the rubbish.

Joyce stifles a cry of victory. She tries to pull out the keyboard but the power cable is snagged somewhere under the garbage bags. She clamps the flashlight between her teeth, jumps inside the container and dives up to her belt in the leftovers from a department meeting: rotting pastry and sodden paper cups. An odour of sour milk leaks out of the bags with a whistling sound.

Joyce swallows her saliva and plunges her hand below the trash.

At the other end of the cable she can feel the cold edges of a computer. The stench of sour milk grows stronger. She holds her breath and sets about clearing a path through the bags. After a long while, the machine emerges from the plastic like a slippery fetus.

Joyce takes a firm hold and hauls it up to the surface. She is exhausted, and lets herself drop back into the garbage so that she can catch her breath. She feels nauseous from the excitement and the methane, but it does not matter—she has finally caught one.

She lifts the computer out of the dumpster and, down on her knees on the asphalt, inspects it more closely. It's an old, battered Texas Instruments 8086 with neither a cover nor a hard disk. Not the big jackpot, but a good beginning.

"Stay where you are!"

She turns around. A paunchy security guard is coming toward her, stroking the handle of his nightstick. Without giving it a second thought, Joyce leaps to her feet. The guard attempts to block her way, but she easily gets around him and dashes toward the exit. Bad luck: another gorilla is in position there—tall, thin, truncheon-wielding, twenty years old, aggressive-looking.

Joyce stops cold. Behind her, the paunchy guard is closing in at a fast trot.

Laurel and Hardy, armed and dangerous.

Joyce's brain is operating at full tilt, every circuit abuzz with electricity. In a few seconds she will be pinned face down on the asphalt, a knee pressed into her back, and duly handcuffed.

She swings around 90 degrees and bolts toward the wire lattice. A Frost fence. Good—she knows how this thing works. She grabs the steel mesh and scrambles up as fast as she can. Too late. A pair of hands are clutching the cuffs of her jeans and pulling her down toward solid ground. She tightens her grip and kicks out blindly. The young, aggressive guard howls with pain and lets go.

Suddenly released from his grasp, Joyce describes an elegant arc over the grid. Sailing head down through the air, she wonders how this is all going to end.

She lands on the grating of the building's ventilation system, the tepid breath of fifty floors of office space: dusty carpeting, overheated plastic, ozone, carbon monoxide, minute particles of paper and keratin. She shakily gets to her feet and yanks off her glove. She has gashed three fingers going over the top of the fence. In the middle of her blood-soaked palm, her lifeline and her fate line trace out a scarlet π.

She inhales deeply and darts toward the street. The metallic echo of her boots ricochets through the depths of the ventilation system five floors below. She hops over a parapet and into the decorative sumac in the flowerbed, comes out on the sidewalk and collides with a vagrant who is pushing a shopping cart filled with aluminum cans.

The vagrant straightens his Toronto Maple Leafs tuque, gives Joyce the once-over and, without saying a word, continues on his way, as solemn as a judge.

Joyce makes off in the opposite direction.

An hour later, sitting on the tile floor of her bathroom, she swabs her wounds with iodine and draws lessons from tonight: she's got to be more careful about surveillance cameras, blind spots and emergency exits.

Another dab of iodine, and no time for tears; her next fishing expedition will take place tomorrow night.

She sticks on one more adhesive bandage and glances at her watch. Two-fifteen a.m. Time to get some sleep. Her workday at the fish store begins in only a few hours.

Thousands of Kilometres

THE CLOCK ON THE MICROWAVE says four a.m. Noah, who has never experienced insomnia before, is discovering this new phenomenon with the same eager excitement he has felt ever since arriving in Montreal.

Sitting at the kitchen table, he writes a letter to Sarah.

His first letter came back yesterday afternoon with an *Unclaimed* notice stamped across the envelope. Strike one. He unceremoniously chucked it into the garbage and immediately sat down at the table to write a new chapter in his new life. He explains that his room is far too large, that he eats fish every day and sleeps among starfish every night, that he is learning Spanish from Maelo and exploring the neighbourhood on an old modified CCM.

Noah closes with an invitation for Sarah to come visit him as soon as she is able. He smiles as he pictures the old trailer moored near the Jean-Talon market. The image is absurd and improbable.

Before sealing the envelope he rereads his letter one last time. His handwriting is as illegible as Jonas's, but there is nothing to be done. He frowns, signs his name and then spreads his road maps out on the kitchen table. Here he is, faced once again with that old problem: in the last five weeks his mother may have covered thousands of kilometres, turned back, stopped in dozens of towns. If he does not succeed in locating her this time around, the probability of finding her again will be approaching zero.

Better apply his new method. Eyes closed, he aims at the map of Manitoba. His index finger harpoons a little village called Notre-Dame-de-Lourdes. He scrawls the address on the envelope, thinking that, all things considered, this place name holds out the promise of a miracle.

Little Italy is asleep. A few wakeful Moroccans are working at the stalls of Jean-Talon market. Noah walks along the deserted streets until he locates a mailbox near Dante Park. The mailbox is almost empty and the envelope hits the bottom with a light metallic tap. He closes the lid very softly, so as not to disturb the unreal silence of the neighbourhood.

He watches the sky growing blue over St-Laurent Boulevard. He ought to get some sleep. In a few hours he will have to confront a new peril: AR-10342, a course called Methodology of Archaeological Studies.

1990

William Kidd

At the request of Robert Bourassa, the armed forces have dismantled the barricades at Kanesatake. The pine grove is crawling with soldiers and journalists, and a small group of Warriors who have fallen back to the reservation detox centre wait to see how events will play out. The situation is confused. International observers fear that this is an incipient Guatemala.

Joyce listens to the reports distractedly. Hunched over the circuits of a computer, she adjusts a few connections with the manic precision of a brain surgeon. Using a felt pen, she writes a name on the machine's dented shell: William Kidd (No. 43).

Hunting down a computer was not easy. Joyce spent weeks of sleepless nights combing the business district. She scoured hundreds of bins, split open thousands of bags, endured countless stenches. She sprained her ankle, bumped her head, scraped her elbows. A number of times she came close to being nabbed by security guards. She ran, climbed, crawled. Worn out and limping, she lugged the precious carcasses from one end of town to the other in the small hours of the morning.

Now, her tiny apartment looks like a bazaar. Everywhere there are piles of broken-down computers, display screens smudged with fingerprints, keyboards with missing teeth, modems, printers, hard disks, floppies, fragments of printed circuits—all of it crowned with a hodgepodge of electric wires and colonies of mice. All of it so obsolete, so covered in grime, that Joyce often feels she has stepped into the shoes of an archaeologist.

Equipped with various handbooks and a screwdriver, she dissects the cadavers, salvages the best organs and grafts them together into a single machine. Lacking the instruments needed to test the condition of each part, she is obliged to proceed by trial and error—and there are many, *many* errors. With each attempt, a new surprise lies in wait. The computer pretends to work, works, then stops working. The power supply spews out smoke and sparks. The motherboard sizzles like a trout in a frying pan. Printed circuits explode, transistors flying in all directions. After being subjected to this merciless treatment, most of the machines are quickly sent back to the garbage heap, with their circuits slightly more charred than before.

Anyone else would have given up long ago. Not Joyce. When she feels herself flagging, she looks at the clipping about Leslie Lynn Doucette tacked to her wall, a little gospel forty lines long. She repeats to herself that she must not doubt, does not have the right to doubt. Faith is a fragile thing. You start by raising some innocuous questions and soon you lose control and throw everything into question: the privation, the sleepless nights, the legendary ancestors, the memories, the hope, the raison d'être.

Better to put your head down and push on without questioning, night after night, printed circuit after printed circuit.

On the radio, the news report is over. "It's 11:07 p.m.," the announcer says, "and you're listening to CBC." Joyce shuts off the radio and anxiously plugs in William Kidd, the forty-third avatar to undergo an attempt at revival. She never knows what to expect. Yesterday, for example, Redbeard (No. 42) blew up due to a premature short circuit, nearly setting fire to the apartment. A few weeks ago, Edward Teach (No. 37) melted down to a compact block of plastic. As for Samuel Bellamy, Francis Drake, François L'Ollonais, and Benjamin Hornigold—No. 03, 09, 13 and 24, respectively—they more prosaically popped all their fuses.

Joyce crosses her fingers, says a brief prayer in memory of Mary Shelley and pushes the switch. After a few seconds, the circuits come to life.

Leaning over the computer's entrails, Joyce listens closely. The power supply's ventilation fan purrs like a tomcat. The BIOS duly enters into action. The RAM sticks seem to be intact. The hard disk boots up flawlessly.

Everything is going too smoothly. Joyce steps back, ready for the worst.

Suddenly, nothing happens.

No explosion, no fizz, no flashes. Only the steady purring of the fan. Incredulous, Joyce watches the cursor blinking on the screen.

William Kidd patiently waits for instructions.

Thomas Saint-Laurent

NOAH HAD JUST FINISHED his third term in archaeology, and was finding it hard to keep the flame alive. Actually, he was convinced that he had left Saskatchewan and travelled thousands of kilometres to study one of the most boring disciplines in the world.

He made a show of finding the courses interesting, but the truth was that digging techniques left him cold, analytical archaeology put him to sleep, and problems of nomenclature seemed to him to be utterly tedious. And as if all that were not enough, he was traumatized by Professor Scott's Indigenous Peoples' Prehistory course.

Edmond Scott came straight out of the nineteenth century. The backbiters even claimed he had personally known the great chief Sitting Bull. Seated in a near-empty auditorium, he had been steadfastly giving the same course since 1969, presenting the panorama of the Algonquins, the Sioux and the Nootkas as though discussing a collection of dead fish floating in jars of alcohol.

This scientific coldness had shaken Noah.

For the first time in ages, he had thought of the old, wrinkled Chipewyans who haunted his mother's trailer. He recalled with disturbing accuracy all the names of the reservations, the convolutions of his genealogy and the finer points of the Indian Act. This approximate, patchwork knowledge, redolent of hay and engine oil, had no place in the classroom.

Noah was afraid that in taking Edmond Scott's course he was committing an unspeakable betrayal of his Aboriginal origins. He consulted various works on the ethics of archaeology, but there was no mention anywhere of such conflicts of interest. He would have to deal with his scruples on his own.

He was toying with the possibility of dropping out of university when a friend advised him to register for Thomas Saint-Laurent's course, which, he said, was "the one course you would have to take if there was only one course to take before the end of the world."

Naturally, Noah had heard of Thomas Saint-Laurent, an enigmatic character who specialized in the archaeology of trash. His résumé was impressive: full professor of archaeology, head of one of the most prestigious research centres in the country, in charge of digs on a number of major prehistoric sites in Nunavik, and author of a dozen books. As well, his work on garbage dumps had been the subject of numerous articles, three documentaries and several television reports.

Among Canadian archaeologists, Thomas Saint-Laurent was the one with the highest media profile, thanks to trash.

Saint-Laurent's colleagues were far from unanimous in approving of this bizarre specialization. Some of them accused him of fomenting rebellion in an already divided faculty, of upstaging his colleagues with his sensational press releases, and of instilling in his students a distorted image of archaeology.

Saint-Laurent himself could not care less. He continued to frequent the dumps and alleyways, to write articles on post-industrial archaeology and to train the next generation of researchers.

The course that Noah signed up for (Order and Disorder: A New Reading of Sedentarism) began with two key principles:

1. Everything is garbage.
2. The study of archaeology began last night at the supper table.

In the months that followed, Noah discovered the stratigraphy of waste-disposal sites, the history of garbage collecting, the expansion of North American suburbs and the petroleum polymer industry. He studied the influence of the Hudson's Bay Company on the lifestyle of the Inuit. He dissected the contents of garbage bags. He compared the fluctuations of the TSE

300 with the increased volume of domestic trash in the suburbs of Toronto.

His view of the world was turned upside down.

Which explains why he has mustered all his courage and, like an unworthy son nervously preparing to ask for his father's blessing, has come to Thomas Saint-Laurent's office to make known his intention of pursuing an M.A. in archaeology under his direction.

"That's great!" Thomas Saint-Laurent exclaims gleefully. "And which subject are you planning on working on?"

"I was thinking of comparing the development of the road network and the expansion of refuse dumps in the 1970s."

A brief pause. Thomas Saint-Laurent nods his head thoughtfully.

"A very exciting project, but a very bad idea. Even if your approach is brilliant and your methods are irreproachably logical, it wouldn't get past the evaluation committee. They reject all projects concerning garbage dumps. It's a prohibited area."

"But your courses?"

"I'm tolerated because they can't get rid of me. Look, I have a proposal for you. Are you interested in the prehistory of the indigenous peoples?"

"I beg your pardon?" Noah stammers.

"This university is a conservative institution. To survive you need a respectable specialization. You want to work on garbage dumps? Well, first you have to make the grade in a less contentious area. Indigenous prehistory is an excellent training ground. Besides, I happen to be in need of an assistant!"

Noah can feel his head start to spin. The irony seems to be just too much.

"I adore indigenous prehistory," he hears himself answering.

1994

The Sea Serpents' Floor

NOAH IS ROOTED IN FRONT OF A MAILBOX. He is closely examining the strata of graffiti and stickers covering the sides of it. *Punk's Not Dead* ¡Viva Zapata! *Lose Thirty Pounds in Thirty Days* — messages that go to the heart of North American civilization. He wonders what archaeologists will think when they unearth this mailbox in three thousand years. Will they grasp the function of this object, or will they believe they have found an altar of some obscure, minor sect?

There are pedestrians hurrying by, brushing past him. A bad spot for daydreaming. He wipes the sweat from his forehead and pulls three envelopes out of his shirt pocket. He has written more than five hundred letters to his mother over the last four years, and he knows by heart the postal code of even the smallest post office between Lake of the Woods and Whitehorse. According to his calculations, Sarah must right now be prowling the vicinity of Lesser Slave Lake, so the three letters are addressed to General

Delivery in Little Smoky (TOH 2ZO), Triangle (TOG IEO) and Jean Côté (TOH 2EO).

He throws the letters into the mailbox and crosses the street, wondering what the weather may be like in the southern Yukon. Behind the heavy glass doors of the library the temperature is decidedly Greenlandian. The door closes slowly and the heat wave is soon reduced to a faint simmer on the other side of the glass.

Noah crosses the deserted hall and passes the book-loan counter, where the clerk is reading *La Route d'Altamont*. Near the photocopiers he chances upon a big bearded man occupied with some strange business. He has emptied the recycling bin onto the floor and is in the process of arranging hundreds of spoiled photo-copies into different piles.

"Tom Saint-Laurent!" Noah cries out happily. "What are you doing?"

"Well, as you can see, I'm analyzing the recycling bins."

"I thought you were in the Laurentians on a fishing trip."

"I was," he confirms, with a troubled look. "But wouldn't you know it, yesterday afternoon, while I was waiting for the trout to bite, I began to think about paper. Have you ever asked yourself what ratio of information these recycling bins contain? What it is that people photocopy? What they throw away and why? What proportion of virgin paper goes directly into recycling?"

He waves a thick stack of paper that has gone through the viscera of the photocopy machines without receiving a speck of polymer-carbon.

"What fascinating refuse—virgin paper! 'Anti-refuse' would be a more accurate term, seeing how it ends up in the trash without having been used. And not just anti-refuse but 'anti-artifact' too—an object that in itself conveys no information."

"So what you're saying is, you jumped into your four-by-four and drove back to Montreal to do some anti-archaeology in the recycling bins."

"Actually, I was just about bored to tears. Fishing isn't really my thing . . . What about you? What are you doing here in the middle of July?"

"This is the best air conditioning in town," Noah says, leaving Thomas Saint-Laurent to his research and heading up to the fifth floor.

As an apprentice archaeologist, Noah would ordinarily be expected to work in Section EF (American History) or Section G (Geography and Anthropology), but he prefers the tranquility of Section V (Naval Sciences, Travel Narratives and Sea Serpents). Even during the worst end-of-term rush, this forgotten corner on the last floor remains the most underused part of the library. Once the term is over, hardly anyone ever goes there—not even a librarian or a janitor—and you can spend weeks there without meeting another soul. No busybodies or snoops or spies. You're free to gaze at the ceiling and daydream, scribble a few poems, doze off on the table, read anything you like any way you like, including shirtless.

Noah has made a personal haven out of a large mahogany table located in the very centre of the floor. For months now he's been leaving his books, papers, pencils and glasses there, as if this piece of furniture were reserved exclusively for his use. But today, quite unexpectedly, Noah finds that a girl has dropped anchor at this very spot.

Stunned, he stands motionless. He glances around in every direction. The floor is deserted, a veritable Sahara of empty tables. Why has this girl chosen to sit *right there* and not somewhere else? Noah becomes suddenly aware of harbouring certain territorial instincts, a paradoxical feeling for someone who was raised at an average speed of sixty kilometres per hour.

Why has he become so attached to this table?

If Sarah were to pop up, like a genie rising out of an old silvery trailer, she would advise him simply to share the space with the girl, or else to collect his books and go colonize another corner of the library. After all, there are four more floors available, not counting the stairwells, the closets and the washrooms. But Sarah isn't there, and Noah approaches gingerly, wondering what the best way to handle this might be. Make himself at home? Beat a retreat? Fake indifference? Act like a tormented intellectual? Claim his territory?

He sits down.

No reaction. The table floats on a sea of silence. Noah fidgets in his chair and coughs. The girl finally looks at him, greets him with a brief smile and immediately reimmerses herself in her reading.

Okay, Noah soberly says to himself.

While pretending to sort his papers, he observes his new neighbour. She has long black hair, somewhat almond-shaped eyes, and little reading glasses. A model student. She has scattered a number of bulky volumes over her territory: *La souveraineté canadienne dans le Grand Nord*, *The High Arctic Relocation*, *Culture inuit et politique internationale*. Clearly, no one on this floor takes the least interest in sea serpents.

The day passes uneventfully. Noah reads, or rather, Noah pretends to read, unable to take his eyes off the girl's olive-skinned forearms, her angular wrists, her restless hand penning what looks like old Italian, backwards, in a small notebook. "A lefty!" he thinks jovially.

A little before noon, the stranger goes away, leaving her things behind. Noah watches her disappear behind the stacks, hesitates for a moment and then grabs the notebook. To his great surprise, everything is written in Spanish. Noah can't help smiling.

A Spanish-speaking student doing research on the Far North in the Naval Sciences section?

Well, why not?

After that, the girl arrives every morning with the regularity of a celestial event. At eight a.m. she walks through the library's glass doors and sits down at an Internet station. She reads the international news, paying special attention to South America and Chiapas, and jots down some notes in her little spiral notebook.

At eight-thirty she consults the library catalogue and transforms the issues she wants to focus on that day into bibliographical citations. Then she crisscrosses the library, moving from one section to another with a pile of books rapidly growing in her arms.

At around eight forty-five, she comes to Section V with her loot. She piles the books on the table, puts on her glasses as though she were putting on a diving suit, and plunges into her reading.

When Noah shows up, fifteen minutes later, all that can be seen of the girl are the air bubbles frothing at the surface. She gets up from her chair only to renew her supply of books, to stretch or to get a quick sandwich in the basement cafeteria.

She keeps up her marathon until she is driven out by the closing bell at eight forty-five p.m., at which point she disappears from the surface of the planet, apparently sucked into the void, only to be returned to the real world the next morning, when the library reopens.

The lapse between nine p.m. and eight a.m. is the Bermuda Triangle.

The days roll by. Noah and the girl still share the big mahogany table. Little by little, the boundary lines between their territories have blurred. Their books mingle and a tacit familiarity arises, made up of silences, rustling sounds and discreet glances. After a week, Noah finds it natural to ask her, "So, what are you working on?"

The girl lifts her nose out of her book and glances around, blinking her eyes as though she were taking her first break in six months.

"The relocations in the remote Arctic."

Five accents are interwoven in these six words: the haughty tone of the Caracas bourgeoisie, the diphthongal speech of Montreal, the haste of Madrid, the nasal intonation of New York and some traces of a recent visit to Chiapas. Where could she be from?!

"Relocations?" Noah asks, with the deliberate aim of hearing that indefinable accent once again.

Arching her back, she yawns slowly.

"Does Inukjuak mean anything to you?"

"It's an Inuit village on Hudson Bay, isn't it?"

"Precisely. In 1953, the Canadian government relocated a number of families from Inukjuak to two artificial villages: Resolute and Grise Fiord. Near the seventy-fifth parallel. So far north that in December the sun stops coming up."

"Why were they relocated?"

"Because of famine. That, at any rate, was the official reason. Last year, the Makivik Corporation filed a complaint with the Royal Commission on Aboriginal Peoples. They claim famine was a pretext. The government only wanted to shore up its sovereignty in the Far North . . . What is it? Why are you smiling?"

"It's nothing."

"You have an opinion on the subject?"

"It seems like the deportation of the Acadians in reverse."

"That's a funny sort of opinion."

"What about you, what do you think?"

"I think it's complicated."

"What were the Royal Commission's conclusions?"

"They ruled in favour of the Inuit, but that doesn't mean anything. The whole thing's very political. There could be royal commissions for all sorts of things that have happened in the south—the Mirabel expropriations, the cutback in services for outlying regions, the closing down of Schefferville . . . But the stakes are different when it comes to Whites."

"Different in what way?"

"Traditional territory."

Noah folds his arms with a skeptical look on his face.

"Okay, wait a second," he says. "Before the arrival of the Whites, the Inuits moved around in step with the game and the seasons. Almost all of today's villages gradually took shape around the Hudson's Bay Company trading posts. Which means that when the families of Inukjuak were relocated, they had been sedentary for no more than two or three generations. So does it still make sense to talk about traditional territory, when the way that territory is occupied now is anything but traditional?"

"Of course! Territory isn't measured in square kilometres. You also have to consider ancestors, posterity, the oral tradition, snowmobile trails, family ties, the seal hunt and the salmon fishery, lichen, legal actions against Hydro-Québec. Above all, territory is a matter of identity."

Noah nods his head without speaking. The girl rubs her eyes and abruptly changes the subject.

"What about you? What's your field?"

"Archaeology."

"And you're interested in the indigenous people?"

"Actually, I'm interested in trash, but . . ."

"Trash?" she says, surprised. "Why trash?"

"It's all about traditional territory."

"I don't see the connection."

"As a rule, archaeologists don't take much interest in nomads. The more a population travels, the fewer traces it leaves behind. They prefer to study civilizations that settle down, that build cities and produce large amounts of garbage. There's nothing more interesting than garbage. Garbage teaches us more than infrastructures, buildings or monuments. Garbage reveals what everything else tries to hide."

"And how does traditional territory fit into all this?"

"The Inuit had no idea what a dump was before the arrival of the Hudson's Bay Company."

The girl nods her head and sizes Noah up with an approving smile.

Her name is Arizna Burgos Mendez, and that is all Noah manages to get out of her. For although she has no qualms about holding forth on the major Aboriginal issues, she immediately cuts short any discussion of a personal nature. This reticence arouses Noah's curiosity, and he sets about deploying all the tactics of a Sioux archaeologist. From harmless discussions and trick questions, he manages to sketch a rough composite portrait.

Arizna was born in Caracas. She was raised by her grandfather, who currently holds an unspecified (but important) position at the Venezuelan consulate in Montreal. She left Caracas at a very early age, lived by turns in New York, Paris, Brussels, Madrid and Montreal, depending on her grandfather's assignments. After several years in Montreal, she returned to Venezuela to study at the Instituto Indigenista Autónomo, a small, little-known university in Caracas. She is interested exclusively in Indigenous studies, is quite willing to discuss the Zapatistas, often scratches her right eyebrow, likes her coffee very sweet and seems to subsist mainly on lentil salad.

Intrigued by this mysterious Instituto Indigenista Autónomo, Noah deepens his investigation. He searches through the library catalogues, combs the Internet, questions Thomas Saint-Laurent—to no avail. There is no mention anywhere of this enigmatic institution. Noah believes the university may be bogus. One morning he decides to broach the question head-on:

Q: So, you're doing your doctorate?
A: No, not really. My university doesn't grant
   diplomas.
Q: Well, which program are you in exactly?
A: There are no programs as such. The students
   follow a general curriculum of variable
   length. Once that's completed they join a
   research group.
   In my case, for example, I'm a member of the
   G.E.T.: the Grupo de Estudio Tortuga, which
   is simply referred to as *la Tortuga*.

Q: And what's the focus of your research?
A: Liberation anthropology.
Q: Meaning what?

The last Q does not receive a satisfactory A. Visibly embarrassed, Arizna stammers a few incredibly vague sentences on indigenism, Venezuela's domestic policies, and a certain Gustavo Gutiérrez—before finally claiming that the concept is hard to translate into French.

Convinced that the answer would be no clearer in Spanish, Noah refrains from asking for a translation. Instead, he slips off in the direction of the library's computer terminals, where he enters: "*anthropology +liberation*." No results. He scratches his chin and enters *Gutierrez, Gustavo*. The computer immediately produces about fifteen titles, including *Liberation Theology*. Noah memorizes the catalogue code and runs to the stacks.

Sheltered in a dark corner of Section B (Philosophy, Psychology and Religion), he leafs through the book without quite knowing what he's looking for. He was brought up without the slightest concept of religion. He couldn't say if his mother was animist, Roman Catholic or Seventh-day Adventist. As a result, he knows as much about religion as he does about the history of the Caucasus in the sixteenth century.

Gustavo Gutiérrez's book makes no mention of indigenism. On the other hand, Noah does discover some unexpected words, which glimmer like cactus needles: *struggle against the domination of the rich, permanent cultural revolution, radical commitment, opulence, injustice, break with society as it exists today, guerrillas.*

Noah closes the book, more bewildered than ever. He comes to a decision: he must meet Arizna between nine p.m. and eight a.m., right in the middle of the Bermuda Triangle.

Jututo

ARIZNA COMES LATE, carrying an expensive bottle of rum under her arm, visibly thrilled at the prospect of taking part in one these famous *jututos*. She kisses Noah on the cheek and thanks him again for the invitation.

"I'm tired of always eating with my grandfather," she explains with a frown.

Right from the first glass of wine, the model student turns into a fearsome polemicist. She takes control of the situation in the time it takes to peel a shrimp. Perfectly at home with familial chaos, she sparks a heated debate on the political future of the Caribbean. Around the table, the guests raise their voices, shake their forefingers and hurl crustacean shells at each other.

The supper is already quite raucous when, after the first bottle of rum has been opened, she stirs up a controversy over the word *jututo*. The term, which for years has been used to refer to this Sunday gathering without ever bothering anyone, suddenly becomes a bone of contention. Everything about the word seems to be controversial, starting with its pronunciation. Cousin Javier asserts that in his village it is pronounced *fu*tuto, Cousin Miguel claims that among the Garifunas of Belize they say *bu*tuto, and Arizna explains that in the Andean countries the preferred pronunciation is *pu*tuto.

Leaving aside phonetics, they try to agree on the nature of the thing itself. Most of the guests affirm that a j(f/p/b)ututo is a trumpet fashioned out of a large shell (of the *Strombidae* family, Arizna specifies), but Cousin Jorge categorically maintains that it is a bull's horn, and Pedro adds that one of his neighbours used a lowly bottle of Brugal which had been broken in half, a procedure he would demonstrate on the spot if not for everyone around the table rushing to stop him.

Which raises the question— as Arizna points out, for the obvious purpose of striking the debate while it's hot—of what the connection is between a Sunday get-together of cousins and a trumpet (be it a shell, a horn or a bottle of rum). Cousin Gina claims the said trumpet once served to sound the village assemblies —hence the metonymy—but this piece of information does not bring them any closer to consensus, and the subject soon becomes the thousand and one potential uses of the *jututo*, each argument being shored up with a generous swig of rum.

After supper, Arizna installs herself in the kitchen, seemingly indifferent to the music, the dancing and the tropical cocktails circulating in the living room. Seated at the table together with four cousins and a suspicious-looking bottle, she talks politics. Uppercut, left jab, hook—she easily demolishes the others' arguments, counters the most complex analyses, makes unexpected assertions and then proves the opposite. When one cousin gives up, another jumps in, as if Arizna, alone against a legion of opponents, were defending her title in a boxing ring marked out by the tablecloth with the fish design.

"Say," Maelo remarks as he brushes by Noah, "your girlfriend, she's a feisty one! Where did you find her—at a karate school?"

"No," Noah replies with a smile, "on the fifth floor of the library."

Toward one a.m., Arizna wriggles out of a sticky discussion on the Organization of American States, wobbles over to the living room and puts her hand on Noah's shoulder. Her voice is still strong, but her eyes are fogging over.

"Everything okay?" she yells over the music.

He nods yes and asks her the same question. Resorting to an inspired bit of sign language, she lets him know that she's had a little too much to drink, and that the ambient blend of sweat, cigar smoke and multiple decibels of cheap *bachata* has given her a nascent twinge of nausea.

Noah guides her to his bedroom and closes the door behind them.

The room, which four years before Noah was afraid he could never fill, is now more crammed than a second-hand store. He has often thought of chucking everything in the garbage so that he could once again experience the delicious dizziness of those early days, but each time he has tried he has come up against the laws of entropy. Matter resists, struggles against, the void. Every bauble suddenly seems to fulfill a vital function, and if, despite this, you venture to throw it away, another bauble with an equivalent volume immediately appears in the empty space.

Noah cannot look at this mess without thinking of his mother. He pictures her in the middle of Saskatchewan, at noon, in a prairie more immense than even the Pacific Ocean. The three thimblefuls of disarray that he could remove from his room seem laughable in comparison with those vast spaces. But those three thimblefuls are all that is missing now for someone to be able to sit down.

Arizna looks around. The only chair is loaded with a pile of books topped with a half-empty cup of coffee and a fan whirling at top speed. She lets herself fall on the mattress, between a stack of *National Geographic*s and an old laptop computer. She takes off her sandals, undoes her belt and taps her stomach.

"Ohhh! Everything is spinning," she sputters. "What do you call that concoction?"

"*Mamajuana.*"

"The roots floating around in the bottle—are they hallucinogenic?" she inquires anxiously.

"No, they just add a bit of a jungle taste to cheap rum. Maelo says it's supposed to be an old Taino recipe."

He rolls up his sleeves and starts to clear the mattress. He stacks the *National Geographic* magazines on the laptop and tries to squeeze the whole lot into a corner of his desk. At the other end of the desk, various piles of papers are on the verge of toppling over. Noah rushes over and catches them just in time. He looks around in search of a few unoccupied cubic centimetres but finds only a glaring lack of cubic centimetres.

He kicks open the closet door, locates a narrow space on the upper shelf, between two cardboard boxes. He tries to push one of the boxes toward the back of the shelf. The box creaks but does not budge.

Noah feels he is losing control of the situation on all fronts. Above him, the box refuses to move. Under his arm, the pile of paper is gradually sliding away. Behind him, Arizna is fighting with the zipper of her jeans and mumbling unintelligible statements about indigenous technologies. He feels he is the prisoner of a concentric series of enclosed spaces: a cardboard box stored in a closet built into a bedroom inside an apartment filled with Dominicans in the process of emptying bottles of rum.

All at once, something cracks dramatically and the box spills its contents onto his head.

"Case closed," Noah mutters, as he brushes the dust from his shoulders.

Arizna, her hand clamped over her mouth, is bursting with laughter. The box's contents have spread at her feet.

"What's this?" she asks, picking up one of the books with her toes.

"Let me see. Oh, that. The Book with No Face. I haven't seen it in years."

"What's it about?"

"Pirates," he says succinctly, dropping down on the mattress beside her. "The same old story. The Spanish steal gold from the Native Indians. The English steal the gold from the Spanish. The Dutch steal the gold from the English."

"How does it end?"

"The Dutch are shipwrecked and the gold ends up at the bottom of the sea."

Her curiosity aroused, Arizna peruses the book. This is the first time Noah has seen her interested in anything but the Indian Act, numbered treaties, the Inuit or the Oka Crisis.

"Interconnected issues," she explains. "Remember, your pirate story begins with the Native Indians' gold."

"That's where their part in the story ends. Native Indians have never been great seafarers."

"Wrong! Have you read *Moby-Dick*?"

"A gap in my education."

"Well, for your information, in the nineteenth century the success of whale-hunting expeditions depended on the skill of the harpooners that got hired on. And the best harpooners were indigenous. There are three in *Moby-Dick*: one is a Native Indian, another is from Oceania and the third is African. They were the most respected members of the crew and they earned the biggest share of the profits. Next to the captain, of course . . ."

She sighs and pops a few more buttons of her blouse while fanning herself with the Book with No Face. Noah wonders how many buttons it takes for a blouse to no longer constitute an enclosed space.

"*Moby-Dick* was written in 1851. That was the golden age of whale oil. After the introduction of fossil fuels, the whaling industry became mechanized. These days, the harpooners of the *Pequod* would be underpaid sailors on a container ship registered in the Bahamas or Liberia."

"That sounds a lot like a pirate story."

"Yes, it does. Can I borrow your book?"

Noah makes a little gesture with his hand as a sign of consent.

On the other side of the wall, the muffled pulsing of the *bachata* diminishes and stops. All that can be heard now are the faint noise of dishes and sporadic conversations. Arizna puts the Book with No Face down on the floor, stretches slowly and looks at her watch.

"Well, that's it," she notes, her voice imbued with implication. "I've missed the last Metro."

Deluge

MONDAY, SEPTEMBER 3, seven-thirty in the morning. Rain is falling for the first time in months. The parched earth refuses to drink it all in and the drains spew back the overflow.

Noah is completely unaware of the weather. He is floating over a field of grain somewhere in Saskatchewan. It is hot and the breeze carves out waves in the barley. After a time, he sinks to the ground, plunges among the golden ears and wakes up in his bed.

He taps the empty space on the port side of the mattress, pokes his head out from under the sheets. Arizna's clothes have disappeared, along with Arizna. Not surprising. Not once since she became a regular at the *jututo* has he managed to wake up beside her.

Resigned, he starts to get out of bed. But when his foot touches down, he discovers to his astonishment ten centimetres of brownish water covering the floor. He rubs his eyes, shakes his head. But the little waves continue to slap against his ankles.

NICOLAS DICKNER

He wades, dumbfounded, through the apartment. A few smelts are swimming around the living room, dreaming of the ocean, while in the corridor various objects limply drift about: three volumes of the *Encyclopédie Cousteau*, an issue of the *Organe des poissonniers*, a pair of shoes.

He discovers Maelo in the bathroom, bailing water into the toilet with a 250-ml measuring cup.

"Has the drainpipe given up on us?" Noah asks casually.

"The drainpipe has given up on us," Maelo answers philosophically.

"What about the landlord?"

"*The party you wish to reach is currently unavailable.*"

Noah watches for a minute as Maelo goes at it, and wonders if his efforts may not be wasted. He leaves the bathroom, half-heartedly perches a few objects above the waterline, then decides to do nothing until the deluge is over. Standing on a chair, he puts on some dry clothes, and navigates toward the front door with his feet wrapped in plastic supermarket bags.

As he leaves the apartment, he comes face to face with the postman. The day's mail amounts to two letters covered with various blue and black seals, and addresses that have dissolved into purple anemones. End results for the summer: His mother did not stop in Little Smoky and there is no post office in Jean Côté.

As for the letter to Triangle, it has apparently vanished into thin air.

Noah dashes into the library, with the downpour close on his heels. The fall term starts tomorrow, and a line of dripping-wet students stretches back from the student loan desk like a throng of disaster victims at a Red Cross field station.

On the fifth floor, the Naval Sciences section is deserted.

Noah circles the table several times, staring at the emptiness with growing disbelief. Except for a precariously balanced pile of books, there is no trace of Arizna.

The Abyss

~

I MOMENTARILY REAPPEAR in this story on the morning of Monday, September 3, 1994. The details are pointless and my intrusion will go unnoticed, over-shadowed by the equinoctial storm that is descending on Montreal three weeks ahead of time. Outside the bookstore, ten million litres of water are cooling the asphalt of St-Laurent Boulevard in a vast hiss of steam.

This staggering low-pressure system is in proportion to the heat wave that preceded it. Two weeks earlier, the thermometer rose to over 50 degrees Celsius, an absolute record after which we stopped keeping track, the mercury having erupted from its glass column. Now fall has arrived—an abrupt, cataclysmic fall. Twirling my thumbs, I look at the water etching sea serpents on the windowpane while I wait for improbable clients. For who would be insane enough to risk his neck by coming here on this end-of-the-world Monday?

Just then, the little bell over the front door, apparently wishing to prove me wrong, chimes out. I immediately recognize the raincoat with the blackened seams and the old blue sailor's duffel bag. A regular customer. She nervously pulls back her hood and fluffs her short-cropped hair. I greet her with a little wave. She answers with a smile.

I've often tried to get acquainted with this mysterious client, to no avail. She smiles politely but forestalls any attempt at familiarity. I don't even know her first name. I should mention that I've always found it hard to establish ties with people. It seems I'm too withdrawn, too much of a homebody. None of my very few lovers was ever able to understand why I was content to make a living selling books. Sooner or later they would end up asking themselves—and, inevitably, asking *me*—why I didn't want to travel, study, pursue a career, earn a better salary. There are no simple answers to these questions. Most people have clearly defined opinions on the subject of free will: Fate (no matter what you call it) either exists or does not exist. There can be no approximations, no in-betweens. I find this hypothesis reductive. In my view, fate is like intelligence, or beauty, or type z+ lymphocytes—some individuals have a greater supply than others. I, for one, suffer from a deficiency; I am a clerk in a bookstore whose life is devoid of complications or a storyline of its own. My life is governed by the attraction of books. The weak magnetic field of my fate is distorted by those thousands of fates more powerful and more interesting than my own.

While this may not be a very attractive appraisal of my situation, at least I can't be accused of being pretentious.

The girl unbuttons her raincoat, wipes her glasses on her sweater and heads toward the computer section. I've never seen her show an interest in any section other than Cooking or Computers. In the first section, she buys all the best books on fish and seafood. In the second, she unobtrusively hides her books under her arm, behind her belt, against her back. Perhaps she thinks of computers as a nasty habit. I've been on to her for a long time, but I pretend not to notice. There are certain thieves one would prefer to stay in touch with.

In order to give her a free hand, I decide to go do a little housekeeping in the Abyss.

Every bookseller cherishes a favourite lost cause. Mine involves arranging the dark little storeroom where for decades my predecessors would toss unclassifiable books pell-mell (before quickly slamming the door behind them for fear of an avalanche). This long accumulation, resulting from denial and procrastination, became the *id* of the bookstore—its unconscious, its hidden face, its unspeakable and chaotic cesspool—in a word, the Abyss.

It has been four years since I began to devote my free time to the psychoanalysis of this incredible place, an undertaking which, in reality, involves digging my way through layers of compressed paper. Progress is slow, as I can work only when the bookstore is deserted. What's more, I must interrupt my labours for three months every year, between June and August, because the thick mantle of mineral wool that insulates this former cold-storage room makes it unendurable.

On the door, an unknown hand has carved a pompous warning: *Abandon all hope ye who enter here.*

Inside, the stifling air smells of warm tow. I sit down on a pile of *People's Almanac* and inspect the environs. The excavation site is as I left it last May. There's even a little yellow bookmark indicating the stack of books I was working on. I look at the backs of these tomes. Typical unclassifiables: an *Atlas of Whale Geometry*, a *Catalogue of Familiar Objects* and the *Directory of Potential Poets in Ungava*. As soon as I budge the stack, a bundle of old *National Geographic* maps drops on my head.

I examine them as I rub my skull. I could, of course, put each of them back in its corresponding issue, but the operation would require several days—a questionable use of my time, considering that we retail issues of *National Geographic* at twenty-five cents apiece and that, in spite of this ridiculous price, we haven't sold even one in the last five years.

I unfold the top map. It is a stereographic projection of the Caribbean titled *Migrations of the Garifunas*. The Garifunas? Never heard of them. They are apparently great voyagers, judging from the complex network of routes that start in South America and South Africa, converge on St. Vincent and the Grenadines, head off again toward Jamaica and finally scatter throughout Central America in a multitude of detours, loops and dead ends.

I hear the girl moving back across the bookstore, betrayed by the creaking floorboards. I emerge from the Abyss, holding my map of the Garifunas.

"Find everything you were looking for?"

She shakes her head with an ambivalent little smile on her lips. People underestimate the X-ray vision of booksellers. I detect a C++ programming handbook hidden under her old raincoat, in the crook of her arm, where it's warm. Lucky book.

I prepare to dive back into the Abyss with my map of the Garifunas when a second brave customer bursts out of the storm and crosses paths with my thief in the doorway. She shakes out her umbrella and looks around. After a moment's hesitation, she throws her umbrella against the Mickey Spillane bookcase and steps firmly in my direction. Her face is somehow familiar, but she is not a regular of the bookshop. A former classmate? Some obscure TV weather reporter? An anonymous resident of the neighbourhood?

She greets me with a little nod and slaps what was once a book on the counter.

"I'm looking for an intact copy of this book."

She has an odd Spanish accent, a voice that means business. Where *have* I seen her? I wipe my hands on my thighs, pick up the book and leaf through it. The back and the cover have been brutally torn away, along with a handful of pages. There is no way to ascertain the title or the author's name, crucial information gone adrift together with the flyleaf. I lay the book down on the counter.

"What's it about?"

"Treasures. Pirates."

"Well, have a look in the Tales of Travel and Adventure section. At the back, on your right, near the washroom. Follow the sound of the leaking faucet."

She heads to the back of the bookstore. I absently study the migratory map of the Garifunas, but am in fact preoccupied by this girl's face. Cashier at the local convenience store? Distant acquaintance once met at a dinner? Fleeting passenger on the No. 55 bus? A bookseller must remember so many things and, as old Borges would say, one unavoidably ends up confusing what one has read, seen and experienced.

The girl's search does not last very long. After ten minutes or so, she walks back to the cash register.

"Find what you were looking for?"

"Even better."

She deposits half a dozen books on the counter, mostly rare books impossible to find in an ordinary bookstore. I dig up a pencil stub and add up the price. The girl hesitantly examines me out of the corner of her eye.

"What's that object around your neck?" she finally inquires.

"A Nikolski compass."

She does not press the point, and looks off in the direction of the Mickey Spillane section. I scribble the total amount of the sale on a bill and hand her the copy.

"That will be $119 all told. Or in round numbers, $110."

I reach under the counter and fish out a large yellow bag from a shoe store. Many clients are surprised that we use recycled bags, but Mme Dubeau maintains that second-hand books must not be wrapped in new plastic.

The girl takes out her wallet and pays without batting an eyelash. She picks up the bag and her umbrella, says goodbye and steps back out into the storm. For a few more seconds, I try to think where I might have seen her before. At the local café? At the Jean-Talon market? On the front porch of an evangelical church? I shrug my shoulders, and am about to go back to the Abyss when I spot her old book with no cover lying abandoned on the counter.

I grab the book and rush out to the sidewalk, search all around, my eyes squinting against the rain. The girl has vanished. I wipe away the water streaming down my neck and run back inside.

Alone with the book, I set about examining it in detail. It seems to be older than it looked at first blush. I open it to the exact middle and read the first sentence that I come upon:

153

Whenever a pirate envisioned in his sleep the hour of his death, he would not dream of going to Heaven but of finally returning to Providence Island.

Pirate stories. Such an odd idea, when you think of it. Why would an author want to devote himself to such a tired old topic? It was surely written by someone like me: a bookworm who never risked getting his slippers wet in the wide world, but preferred to live the buccaneer's life of roaming and adventure vicariously. I give the book a thorough inspection but can find absolutely no trace of the author's name. Nothing but an old, dismembered text, written by a faceless man.

Then I notice a curious detail: the typeface on the first and last pages is inconsistent. On closer examination I see that the typography and the width of the margins are also different. There are imperfections in the seams, variations of colour and texture in the paper. And then in a flash I realize the truth. The book is actually composed of a set of fascicles taken from several books and roughly cut and bound together.

By following the strange pagination, I easily manage to identify the fragments of three works, appearing in the following order:

Pages 27 to 54: a very old monograph on treasure islands;

Pages 71 to 102: a vaguely historical treatise on the pirates of the Caribbean;

Pages 37 to 62: a biography of Alexander Selkirk, castaway on a desert island.

This enigmatic book assembles, under the anonymity of a single binding—or what's left of it—three destinies once scattered over various libraries, or even over various garbage dumps. Which leaves outstanding the question as to what sort of twisted mind could have conceived of such an amalgamation, and to what end.

For now, I wonder if the girl will come back looking for her three-headed book. If she neglects to, we could naturally consider it ours and put it up for sale. But it would be impossible to sell this curiosity. In its present state it would be worth no more than fifty cents, and one can't surrender books for fifty cents. It would be irresponsible.

I look at the book with budding affection. I wrap it carefully and store it away in my backpack.

Never One Degree Off

⌒

THE AWAKENING IS SO RUDE that I sit up in my bed with a jolt. I turn on the lamp and rub my eyes vigorously. A teapot, the Three-Headed Book and the Nikolski compass come into view on the night table. The alarm clock says 2:07 a.m.

I finally remember where I saw the stranger in the bookstore.

The story goes back to August 1992. I was keenly following the events of the Oka Crisis, especially since the Warriors of the Kahnawake Reservation had barricaded the Mercier Bridge, less than ten minutes from my hometown. From time to time, I would see a former neighbour busy insulting the police or the Indians, or both at once.

I had caught sight of the girl in the background of several news reports, mingling inconspicuously with the journalists in the Kanesatake pine grove. She was young, pretty, dressed in a khaki shirt and a pair of jeans. She did not wear a bulletproof vest, but a press card hung from her neck. I spotted her because of her black hair, which was long and straight, her olive-coloured skin, and her eyes, which, in spite of the distance, I pictured as slightly almond-shaped. She looked to be Native, and I was repeatedly surprised to see her among the journalists and the police rather than on the side of the insurgents. The Aboriginals must surely have been everywhere on both sides of the barricades— as advisers, negotiators, human rights observers—but, oddly, this girl seemed out of her element to me.

Sitting in my bed, I shuffle through these distant images, trying to connect them with the unknown girl's visit to our bookstore. Was it a coincidence, or is there an invisible link between the internal politics of Kanesatake and the battered old book full of pirate stories?

And that is exactly the trouble with inexplicable events. You inevitably end up interpreting them in terms of predestination, or magic realism, or government plots.

I glance at the Nikolski compass and gently tap the plastic three times with my knuckles, the way one would hit the glass of a barometer. The globe oscillates and obstinately returns to 34° W. Never one degree off. Go figure.

I switch off the light and try to go back to sleep.

1995

Stevenson Island

THE SUN WON'T BE COMING UP for another twenty minutes or so in this forsaken corner of the northern hemisphere. Glittering at the bottom of the bay is the cluster of electric bulbs of Tête-à-la-Baleine. The red and green navigation lights of a cod-fishing boat work their way up the channel, sail past the Îles Mermettes lighthouse and disappear behind Providence Island.

Noah shivers as he watches the ghostly bulk of an iceberg drifting offshore. Eight hundred nautical miles downriver from Montreal the month of May is anything but springlike, and he wonders if this rocky, frozen island actually represents an improvement over Section V at the library.

He adjusts his tuque and walks back up to the excavation site.

Despite its rather ambitious name, all the *site* consists of is four old yellow nylon tents standing in a random arrangement, a sifter suspended between three trimmed spruce trees, several dozen plastic containers of various sizes, and a latrine knocked together out of an old military tarpaulin and a theodolite tripod, all of it overlooked by the compact mass of the Bunker. And directly to the rear, where the main dig is located, Howard and Edward are beavering away.

When they aren't fighting over the coffee Thermos, these two characters are busy unearthing an ancient Inuit gravesite—a circle of stones in the centre of which a gnawed skeleton is heaped up in a vaguely fetal position. The bones emerge from the humus a millimetre at a time, to the beat of countless tiny brush strokes. A thousand years earlier, an old nomad lay down in this circle of stone to finally put an end to his migrations. His soul and his carbon-14 were carried off by the wind, but his bones have not moved since then.

Noah walks quietly around the Bunker and heads toward the second dig, which is his personal assignment. This site is a kind of prehistoric campground, and the challenge is to reconstruct the campers' identities and their way of living on the basis of small scraps of refuse strewn over the landscape. The task is exquisitely complex because, while it is easy to track sedentary populations by following the greasy fingerprints they have smeared all over history, the distant presence of nomads must be construed from next to nothing: a seal-bone hook corroded by the acidity of the ground, traces of charcoal, shells dispersed among the cobbles.

Stevenson Island has seen quite a lot of traffic over the centuries. If you scratch the surface carefully, you discover the stubborn vestiges of fishermen of the Maritime Archaic, Dorset seal hunters, bearded Scandinavians, Thule Inuit, Basque whalers, Naskapis and shipwrecked French mariners—not to mention a small group of archaeologists who haven't showered in two weeks and who get excited over the slightest shard of flint.

Noah kneels down in the trench, rakes the ground with his trowel and collects minute quantities of blackish earth, which he steadily deposits in a plastic bag. Little by little, a constellation of cinders comes to light. A thousand years ago an earthenware jar fell to the ground, toppled perhaps by a restless child. Closing his eyes, Noah could swear he hears an outburst of Paleoinuit curses.

As he notes the position of the cinders in the excavation logbook, Noah hears shouts ringing out by the cairn. He lifts his head above the trench just in time to witness a border skirmish between Howard and Edward. Things are starting to heat up, and soon they're brandishing weapons. Howard tries to crush Edward's skull with his trowel, but Edward—who was a fencer in college—dodges the blow and counters with a miniature garden rake, attempting to drive Howard back into his trench. Noah sighs, throws a last handful of earth into the plastic bag and goes up to the

Bunker without paying any attention to the small clicking noises of battle.

As with any self-respecting bunker, one must bow to enter. Inside, the walls have disappeared behind hundreds of white plastic bags filled with earth. The impression one gets is of a World War One shelter, which in fact is what suggested to Thomas Saint-Laurent the affectionate nickname of his headquarters. But here there are no shells or bullets. The plastic bags are shields against the passage of time. Outside, the twentieth century may roar on, but inside the Bunker the atmosphere has been stabilized at *circa* 500 BCE.

Amid the disorder, a large trestle table sags under the weight of boxes filled with stones, potsherds and piles of cardboard index cards. Seated before an assortment of arrowheads, Thomas Saint-Laurent is coating his arms with DEET.

"What is that noise outside?"

"The daily homicide attempts."

Noah takes a felt pen, numbers his bag of humus and adds it to the Bunker's supporting wall. One more contribution to wartime architecture.

Every night after supper, the work continues by lantern light. They discuss the day's events while washing the dishes, then rewrite their notes and classify whatever is to hand. Then, overcome by the cold, they go to bed early, each in his own tent.

Trussed up in his army-surplus sleeping bag, with his flashlight wedged under his chin, Noah examines the old map of the Caribbean pinned to the tent wall. This is all that's left of the Book with No Face, which vanished at the same time as Arizna. Ten months have gone by since Noah saw either one.

He watches the mist rising from his mouth and thinks of Leonard, a classmate who at this very moment is busy stirring the venerable dust of Hydra in the Saronic Gulf. Noah has the feeling he is on the wrong island. He has thought several times of dropping out of university, but without a satisfactory alternative he could not bring himself to face the real world. And yet here he is, stretched out on a bed of lichen, looking at an old map of the Caribbean, shivering.

The beam from his flashlight, which has been waning for some time, blinks and goes out. Noah gives the flashlight a shake, but in vain. Nothing left to do now but try to get some sleep. Turning over on his side, he notices a glimmer through the nylon of the tent. A light is shining in the Bunker. He wriggles out of his sleeping bag, gets dressed and exits his tent. An icy wind is blowing in from the sea. To the east, the Îles Mermettes lighthouse winks at two-second intervals.

The cold inside the Bunker seems even more severe, and Thomas Saint-Laurent, sitting at the work table, is swathed in three woollen sweaters and, over these, an old patched-up quilt. Surrounded by a swarm of mosquitoes, he is studying the logbook in the hissing light of the butane lamp.

"Well, well," he exclaims, "another insomniac!"

From under the woolly layers he pulls out a stainless steel flask, and throws it over to Noah. Judging by the smells wafting around the bunker, the flask contains either alcohol or insect repellent. Noah unscrews the cap and sniffs.

"Whisky?"

"Scotch," Tom Saint-Laurent replies, stretching. "Cutty Sark, to be more exact."

"The bottle with a sailing ship?"

"The bottle with the *Cutty Sark*. The fastest sailing ship of the nineteenth century. It carried Chinese tea and Australian wool. Now it's in London, and its holds are full of tourists."

Noah takes a swig and sends the flask back to Thomas Saint-Laurent, who in turn takes a drink.

"I thought all boats ended up sinking."

"Not that one."

The temperature in the Bunker rises a notch. Thomas Saint-Laurent rests his feet on the corner of the table, on top of a stack of forms from the Ministry of Culture.

"So, can't get to sleep?"

"I have nightmares. I spend my nights digging holes with a teaspoon."

Noah looks at the hundreds of bags surrounding

them. At the end of the summer, they will have to sift scrupulously through all that earth and retrieve the slightest potsherd that may have escaped their attention, then methodically bury the site while respecting the strata. In September the ground surface will display *165* a few irregularities at most. Next year the lichen will start growing again. In two years, there will be no sign of their passage on Stevenson Island.

"Yup," Tom Saint-Laurent sighs. "Sometimes archaeological digs lack romanticism. And to think that at this moment I could be trout-fishing in the Laurentians . . ."

"Let me remind you that last summer you interrupted your fishing trip to do some digging in the library recycling bins."

"You're right. It's just a convenient image to convey the serenity of summer. A lake, the trout, the mosquitoes."

"You never travel?"

"I don't like to travel alone."

"I thought you were married," Noah says, surprised.

"Divorced, naturally. No one but a divorced man or a crazy bachelor would come out to a deserted island on the Lower North Shore to scratch at the ground. What about you—do you have a girlfriend?"

"No girlfriend. No family either. My mother lives in a trailer. She never stops in the same place for more than two weeks. At this time of year, she must be in Banff. Or Whitehorse."

"No sisters or brothers?"

"None that I'm aware of."

"And your father?"

"My father? Worse than my mother. He used to work on freighters. Couldn't sit still. Last time we had any news, he was living in Alaska. I think he settled on a small Aleutian island."

"Strange place to settle down."

"No worse than Stevenson Island."

There's a moment of silence permeated by the buzzing of mosquitoes. The two archaeologists become lost in their thoughts. After a while, Thomas Saint-Laurent takes a gulp of whisky and tosses the bottle over to Noah.

"I know what you're thinking. You wanted to do your master's on garbage dumps, and now you regret having changed your mind."

"I didn't change my mind. You refused to support my project."

"True," he admits apologetically. "I wanted to spare you the disillusionment. I could have let you draft your project. The admissions committee would have rejected it, and you would have wasted three months on a dead-end road."

"It's okay," Noah answers quietly, as he takes another swallow. "I don't blame you for anything."

Saint-Laurent signals that he'd like to have the Scotch back. He takes a drink.

"I know just how you feel. I've been feeling I'm in the wrong place too. I find this almost as boring as a fishing trip. I'd prefer to spend the summer at the Miron dump. Now, there's a challenge! Have you ever applied for a permit to excavate a dump? It's a real obstacle course. Civil servants mistrust archaeologists. They prefer treasure hunters."

"Treasure hunters?"

"Companies that deal in luxury garbage. Most of them take apart old computers and salvage the metal. They call it waste management."

He sighs, takes a small gulp of whisky and lobs the flask to Noah.

"The fact is that computer recycling is at an impasse. One ton of printed circuits yields a few ounces of gold, so to make a profit you have to handle large volumes of raw material. You have to separate the circuits, the processors, the wiring, the hard drives, the cases. You end up with tons of toxic waste on your hands. It's not easy to make a profit. Too many steps in the process, too much hazardous residue to manage. So you turn a blind eye to the Basel Convention and you export your electronic garbage to Asia."

"The Basel Convention—what's that?"

"Didn't you take my Archaeology and International Politics course?"

"It's been a while."

"The Basel Convention regulates the transportation and processing of waste. Theoretically, it prevents the industrialized countries from exporting their trash to the Third World. The treaty was inaugurated in 1989, not long before the Berlin Wall came down. Conditions were ripe. As soon as the Iron Curtain fell, Western Europe started to export its surplus waste to Poland, Bulgaria, the Ukraine."

"I can't believe they export garbage!"

"The dumps are overflowing. Are you familiar with Fresh Kills?"

"It's a dump in New York, right?"

"The *main* dump of New York. Twelve square kilometres, a yearly increase of over 4 million tons of trash, daily emissions of 2,600 tons of methane. In 1990, William Rathje wanted to do some drilling in Fresh Kills. He rented a drill and cored the garbage. At one hundred feet below the surface the flow of time slows down. No oxygen, no bacteria, no biodegradation. His team brought up a perfectly preserved head of lettuce dating back to 1984. It looked as if it had been thrown in the trash a few days before."

Noah tosses back the whisky. Unaffected by their game of liquid table tennis, Tom Saint-Laurent continues.

"To travel back in time as far as that head of lettuce, Rathje had to get excavation permits, a core-drilling machine, specialized machine operators, different logistical vehicles, and assistants to sort through the artifacts. For the Ministry of Culture, there's no way to make that head of lettuce cost-effective. It's a vegetable with low political potential."

He pauses and grimly inspects the bottom of the flask. "Empty," he grumbles.

He reaches toward a crate and pulls out a brand new bottle of Cutty Sark. He sets about filling the flask, but the repeated swigs have made his hand unsteady. He frowns.

"I know better than anyone that we look like a bunch of nerds with our plastic bags full of humus. But the truth is, we're ahead of our time. Archaeology is the discipline of the future. Every time an old IBM finds its way to the dump, it becomes an artifact. Artifacts are the main products of our civilization. When all the computer experts are unemployed, we'll still have millions of years of work ahead of us. That is the fundamental paradox of archaeology. Our discipline will reach its peak at the end of the world."

Thomas Saint-Laurent has miraculously completed the transfer from bottle to flask without spilling a single drop of the precious Scotch. He screws the bottle shut, returns it to its niche, and addresses Noah with the flask raised in the air.

"In the meantime, the best remedy is patience."

Pigmentation

OF ALL THE FISH THAT JOYCE SEES coming through Shanahan's—from the diminutive capelin to the blue mackerel, winter skate and swordfish, right through to the majestic Northern bluefin tuna—her favourite is the plaice.

This undistinguished *pleuronectida*, neither formidable nor athletic, is matchless in the art of mimicry. Its flattened silhouette and complex epidermal pigmentation allow it to completely blend in with the sea bottom. When immobile, it vanishes. When swimming, it resembles a mere puff of sand stirred up by the current.

The young plaice has an eye on either side of its head. As it grows, its left eye migrates northward and goes to meet the right eye. Thereafter blind on the murky side of its existence, it no longer directs its gaze anywhere but up, as if assuming there must be a surface and, above the surface, another world, the sky, the clouds, the stars.

Joyce is absorbed in her consideration of a plaice when two RCMP officers abruptly enter the fish store.

As soon as she sets eyes on these two hammerheads, Joyce feels her pulse accelerate. The heftier of the two removes his sunglasses and looks around as though he were the store owner.

"Are you still open?"

"I was about to close up," Joyce answers, smiling like a model student. "How can I help you?"

"Do you have any trout?"

"As it happens, the fillets are on special."

"I'll take three."

Joyce wraps the fillets, weighs the package and marks the price on the label. The officer pays, puts his dark glasses back on and goes out. His partner follows without a word, like a pilot fish.

Standing by the window, she watches them climb into their car, parked right in the middle of the loading zone. She flashes a thin smile. Only a slight quiver in her lower lip betrays the pressure she feels inside.

Joyce turns off the lights, puts away the merchandise and rinses the counters with large sloshes of water. A final pass with the mop, and the fish store is ready for the next day. Then she prints out that day's sales on the cash register and, while the paper roll plays itself out, sorts the receipts.

A series of numbers suddenly draws her attention. Joyce can recognize in a single glance the credit card numbers of most of the shop's regular customers. This particular number belongs to some businessman who comes every Tuesday, double-parks his BMW, demands to be served first, berates anyone within earshot and complains about the appearance of the most trivial shrimp, faulting whoever has the misfortune of standing behind the counter at that moment. All the employees of the shop, including the very peaceful Maelo, dream of slicing him into little steaks.

Joyce, deep in thought, fidgets with the receipt. Something rapacious momentarily flickers across her iris. Beneath its lovely freckled skin, the plaice is a predator.

She is about to note the card number in the palm of her hand, hesitates for a long while, then changes her mind. She staples together the receipts and calmly goes on with her calculations. There is a cash overage of $7.56. Joyce puts all the money—including the overage—in the deposit envelope, seals the envelope and slips it into the safe.

After entering the alarm system's activation code, she goes to the door while counting down in her head. Outside, the air is heavy with various smells: carbon monoxide, overheated asphalt, crates of rotten fruit piled up along the edges of Jean-Talon market. Joyce inhales deeply and, taking her time, crosses the street.

The janitor is polishing the building's glass door, his arms moving in broad, fluid strokes; he looks oddly like a cleaner fish suction-cupped to an aquarium wall. He interrupts his work and greets Joyce with a nod—a respectful acknowledgment reserved for honourable, wage-earning citizens.

The fruits of Joyce's most successful piece of camouflage.

Lightning Rod Jim

Available For A Limited Time, Special Offer While Supplies Last, Fall-Winter 1995 Collection, $15 Discount With This Coupon, Made in the U.S.A., Prices in Effect for the Week of 12 September 1995, No Deposit, No Credit Charges, 15% Discount On All Items, Class A, Top Quality, Warehouse Sale, Up To 70% Off On All Clothing, Grand 99¢ Clearance Sale.

Altogether, ten centimetres of glossy paper and newsprint, high-quality printing and colour photos compressed inside clear plastic wrapping. On the geological scale, these ten centimetres would represent centuries or even millennia, but as this is only advertising tossed through the door, Noah dates the whole thing to a mere five days ago—which leads him to the conclusion that Maelo has been away on holiday since last week.

Knapsack slung over his shoulder, sleeping bag rolled under his arm, bearded, smelly, studded with mosquito bites, he has just returned from Stevenson Island and is on a short fuse. He grabs the heap of paper and heads toward the closest garbage pail, sifting through the bundle as he goes. The net result is three bills and two letters addressed to Sarah, which have bounced back from the post offices in Athabasca (T9S 1A0) and Waskatenau (TOA 3P0), respectively. He drifts into the living room as he opens the bills, and turns on the television in passing. There is a news report on the situation in Bosnia-Herzegovina. NATO forces have shelled Serb positions and, in response, the Serbs have bombarded Sarajevo. Noah shuts off the TV with a kick and drops down on the couch. After four months of isolation, he can see the world hasn't changed. Arms spread wide, the Hydro-Québec bill unfolded in his lap, he stares at the ceiling. Last year's floods have left their mark even there. A flourishing colony of fungus has begun to trace petroleum-green atolls across the roughcast.

Noah's thoughts turn to the South Pacific. He would like to be somewhere else but has no idea where.

He casts a weary glance at his watch. Might as well have a shower and head over to the university.

Thomas Saint-Laurent is giving his first course of the term (AR-10495—Activism and Contemporary Archaeology), and Noah finds himself alone in the laboratory, grappling with a grant application.

The office is quiet except for the hum of the computer and the mummy freezer. Noah's eyes are on the monitor but his hands have not yet touched the keyboard. Occasionally, he sniffs the inside of his wrist. The soap has not washed away the resinous tang of Stevenson Island.

He looks at the four walls of the office in search of an excuse to go out. He has a sudden craving for some very strong coffee. In the kitchen, the tiny black-and-white television set is playing with the sound off. As he stirs his coffee, Noah discovers the merits of a revolutionary razor with aloe vera, a diaper with a built-in humidity gauge, and space-age garbage bags. The commercials are interrupted by the four p.m. news bulletin. He is about to return to the office but stops in his tracks.

The screen is completely filled with a close-up of Thomas Saint-Laurent's face. Noah turns the volume all the way up:

> . . . *demonstration at the entrance to the Miron waste-disposal site in Ville St-Michel. For more than an hour, demonstrators prevented employees from entering the site* . . .

A long line of trucks stretches across the screen. Against a backdrop of seagulls, Thomas Saint-Laurent and his crew of about twenty students are waving protest signs that were evidently put together during the practical portion of their course. The camera captures some of the slogans: *Save the refuse!*, *Garbage Dump = Heritage* and *NO to Incineration!*

Noah wonders if slogan-writing will count toward their final grade for the term.

. . . the arrival of a group of environmentalists, who immediately engaged in discussions with the first group of demonstrators . . .

Gesturing with his hands, Thomas Saint-Laurent is enthusiastically explaining the subtleties of his course syllabus to a stocky environmentalist holding a heavy placard. The meeting continues with the demonstrators swinging at each others' placards. A melee ensues. The camera shows a close-up of three sanitation workers nonchalantly leaning on their truck, smoking cigarettes as they watch the scuffle.

. . . MUC police officers quickly intervened and proceeded to make nine arrests.

The spectacular thirty-second report ends as a couple of constables totalling 190 kilos haul away a heroic Thomas Saint-Laurent—black-eyed and bloody-nosed—and bundle him into the back seat of a cruiser, a compelling image immediately followed by a commercial for analgesics.

Noah comes home carrying a case of beer, waging war against the whole damned Western world. He violently kicks the door open, uncaps a beer while standing in the hallway and, without even bothering to remove his coat, is about to knock back the first swig when the telephone stops him in mid-air. He grabs the receiver and barks, "Yes?!" like a raging Mongol warrior.

In response to this terse prelude comes a long, bewildered silence.

"Noah?" Arizna asks tentatively.

Noah feels the tension creeping into every fibre of his muscles, from the inferior peroneal all the way up to the occipital abductor. His spine goes stiff. His fingers tighten around the receiver, squeezing an agonized groan out of the plastic. His mouth is wide open, but nothing comes out.

"Long time no see," she continues, too lightheartedly.

"A year," Noah replies, his voice somehow foreign.

His right hand begins to shake. The tremor travels to his shoulder and continues down to his knees. His teeth are chattering and his skin prickles. And now his entire body feels like a wrecked car tumbling down a jagged slope. He tries to get a grip on himself. *It's been a rough day*, he reasons, wiping his forehead. First coming back to civilization, then Thomas Saint-Laurent's arrest and now Arizna's reappearance. He thinks of the Texas Ranger who was struck three times by lightning. Lightning Rod Jim was his name—a freak of nature. Noah has always wondered how this chubby, ordinary-looking man could have survived three electrocutions.

"Would you like to go out for a drink?" Arizna presses.

The air pops in Noah's ear. He watches the fine spray of gas floating out of the freshly opened beer bottle.

"Well actually, I . . ."

"Excellent!" she exclaims. "I'll be expecting you!"

Noah doesn't have time to say another word. Arizna tells him her room number at a hotel in the heart of the business district, and he's left alone with the one-note hum of the receiver.

The air around him smells of something burning.

Pirates Are Pragmatists

WHEN SHE COMES HOME, Joyce cautiously lifts the lid of a pot she left on the stove and subjects the contents of the pan to an olfactory inspection, before lighting the burner and turning it to low.

Her studio apartment is redolent with the smell of the sea. The kitchen counter is littered with the shapes of her last meals: grilled fish, poached fish, fish soup, shrimp chips. The area around the sink is overflowing with dirty dishes, soiled glasses, encrusted pots. The rest of the room looks much the same, and Joyce ambles through the disorder kicking lightly at the objects scattered on the floor.

The back of the room is taken up by a makeshift desk, built with wood lifted from a construction site. Two computers share this piece of furniture: Jean Lafitte (No. 54), in good working order despite the bruises, and Henry Morgan (No. 52), whose innards are currently exposed. The surrounding area is strewn with electronic remains, screwdrivers, stacks of floppies, piles of old modems. The space beneath the table is crammed with an automatic dialer, an antique fax machine and three boxes full of printed circuits.

The only analog object in the area is a bottle of Saint James. Joyce uncorks it with her teeth and pours herself a glass of rum.

There are two news items pinned to the wall. The first announces the FBI's arrest of Leslie Lynn Doucette. Forty lines, no photo—a pirate with no face. The second, even more concise, is a report on the outcome of the trial: Doucette has been sentenced to twenty-seven months in prison and will lose custody of her two children. The judge's manifest intention in handing down this unduly harsh verdict was to set an example.

These two scraps of yellowing paper make up the entire media coverage of what might have become the Doucette File, but never got beyond the level of the 2,348th fender bender story in the summer of 1989. While computer pirates were beginning to capture the public's imagination—and the attention of the American legal system—Leslie Lynn Doucette was paradoxically relegated to media limbo, somewhere between an oil spill at Dock 39 in New York harbour and a fire at a New Jersey postal outlet. The deskmen apparently felt that a young single mother from the northern suburbs of Chicago was hardly compatible with the mythos of the pirate.

The story's conclusion remains a mystery. Did she sit out all of her twenty-seven months of detention, get time off for good behaviour, or escape by way of the prison's ventilation system? Did she get back custody of her two children? Was she subjected to a special restraining order forbidding her from coming within ten metres of any electronic device? Is she working for minimum wage in a Burger King on North Ridge Boulevard?

Joyce raises her glass to Leslie Lynn. Then she picks up a telephone wire coiled under the table and goes out on the fire escape. She tiptoes to the neighbour's window and peeks in between the curtains. The place is dark. No one home.

The neighbour is a trucker for an oil company. He leaves Montreal every Monday at dawn, drives to Halifax and does not come back before Saturday afternoon. His apartment is unoccupied 80 per cent of the time, and Joyce has taken advantage of this absence to *upgrade* his telephone equipment. Using an electronics handbook she found in a Bell Canada dumpster, she has patched together a small intermediate concentrator and hidden it in the gap between the fire escape and the wall of the building. This clever device allows her to use the neighbour's telephone without worrying about phone bills or RCMP interference.

She connects the wire and goes back into her apartment. She flicks awake Jean Lafitte and, with a serene smile on her lips, listens to the modem yodelling its way toward a connection—the song of a whale adrift in the city.

The modem goes silent again. The connection has been established and Eudora announces the day's tally: *You have 34 new messages*. It will take a while to download them all.

Joyce backs up her chair, takes a sip of rum and turns on the radio. The local news bulletin reports that a rally got out of hand near the Miron waste-disposal site. After they had disrupted the work of the garbagemen for nearly an hour, internal strife erupted among the demonstrators. The group split into two factions and they came to blows. The police, after letting the demonstrators beat each other up for a while, arrested nine individuals. The reasons for the demonstration remain unclear.

An imperative signal from Eudora draws Joyce's attention. She puts down her glass and scans the messages. In most cases, the title and name of the addressee are enough to give away the content of the message: credit card numbers being sent or requested. Business as usual.

She opens her database and composes a few requests. The results twist her face into an annoyed pout. Her supply of numbers has reached the critical level. She has traded practically everything left and right, and it would be imprudent to put off any longer a foray into the financial district to replenish her supplies.

She leans out the window and glances at the sky. There is about an hour left before sunset. She drains her glass, refills it and starts to undress. She pitches her work clothes onto the pile of dirty laundry and pulls on black overalls, a black T-shirt and a scruffy black sweater. From under the bed, she fishes out a pair of black army boots, a flashlight, a pair of black work gloves and Grandfather Doucet's venerable navy-blue duffel bag.

As she gets dressed, Joyce works out a plan of attack. Her brain encloses the entire downtown district, carefully cut up into quadrants, zones and subzones. You don't go fishing for just any old thing, any old where, at any time. The makeup of the trash not only varies from one alley to the next, but depends as well on the season, stock-market trends and U.S. foreign policy.

For Joyce, this is all organized in a complex map. And beneath the surface flows a huge mass of information: memos, passwords, organization charts, cash-register receipts, carbon copies, address books filled with names and telephone numbers, not to mention the hard disks, floppies, magnetic tapes and compact disks. This wealth of data fuels the precision operations that—quite ironically—she later performs on computers salvaged from the very same garbage.

And when the last drop of juice has been extracted, the rinds are discarded in another bin.

While she laces her boots, Joyce wonders what Herménégilde Doucette, the scourge of the New

England coast, would think if he saw his great-great-great-granddaughter preparing a raid on the down-town dumpsters. He would surely approve. Pirates, after all, are pragmatists.

A sweet aroma of fish, cumin and lime is filling up the room. The soup on the stove has begun to simmer.

A Dose of Future

STREET LEVEL. A vagrant wearing a Toronto Maple Leafs hockey tuque pushes a grocery cart loaded with his harvest of empty bottles.

Noah considers with some apprehension the massive door of the hotel. A half-ton of oak and polished brass. As there is no one around, the doorman is busy hustling the cart-pusher out of the line of sight of hotel guests. Noah pulls open the door and lets himself be drawn in by the lobby's vastness. Thick carpets, reproductions of antique furniture, crystal chandeliers—he asks himself what he is doing here. He checks the back of the crumpled grocery slip where he wrote down the room number, and takes the elevator to the top floor.

Arizna apologizes for receiving him in this impersonal penthouse, but she was obliged to take a room at the hotel because her grandfather has moved to Miami.

"He's traded diplomacy for import-export, the old fox."

She pours a Perrier for Noah (who wistfully thinks of his case of beer back home) and sits down opposite him, in a purple Louis XV armchair of some sort. An embarrassed silence settles over the penthouse.

"Your voice on the telephone was odd," she ventures. "Was I bothering you?"

"No," he lies. "Your call surprised me, was all. I thought you were in Venezuela."

"I was. I just arrived."

"You seem to change locations on very short notice. Are you living in Caracas?"

"No, I've moved to Margarita Island. My grand-father has a house there. But I spend most of my time in the capital."

"Are you still a student?"

"Only part-time. I'm working on other projects right now. I'm about to open a publishing house, you know."

A mobile phone starts to vibrate on the table. Arizna excuses herself and, answering in Spanish, expedites something about a contract, meetings and percentages. She looks quite pleased as she puts the cellphone back on the table a minute later. She jots down a few notes on a pad, nods her head and refills Noah's glass.

"So, please, tell me about this publishing house," he says politely.

"It's called Editorial Tortuga."

"Like your research team, right?"

"Yes. Actually, I'll be working in tandem with the Instituto Indigenista. There's no lack of projects. In January we're launching a quarterly on indigenous studies. Followed by the first two titles of our catalogue: a book on Zapatism and alternative economies in March, and then, in the early summer, a textbook on pre-Colombian history."

"You're ambitious. Do you think it will fly?"

"We're crossing our fingers. Our biggest problem is distribution. It involves huge sums of money. For the time being, my grandfather is putting up 75 per cent of the necessary funds."

"Long live import-export," Noah quips, with a wry little smile.

"I know. With some luck, we'll be self-sufficient by next year."

Second interruption—a knock at the door. Arizna rolls her eyes. Evidently, she has spent all day answering the door and the telephone. With a sigh, she gets up to open the door. Standing at attention in the hallway, an obsequious bellhop hands her an "urgent fax." She tips him and shuts the door while skimming the paper. She then tosses it on the table and, rubbing her eyes, comes back to sit facing Noah.

"What about you? Still doing your postgraduate work?"

"Theoretically."

"Now, that's what I call enthusiasm."

"Things aren't working out too well for me these days."

"Didn't you want to do research on garbage dumps?"

"Yes, but I was told my project would be rejected by the admissions committee, so I agreed to work on Native Indian prehistory. The upshot is that I've just spent four deadly months on the Lower North Shore wading through lichen and pebbles. And then, as soon as I get back to Montreal, my research director gets thrown in jail."

"Really?" she says, suddenly expressing interest. "In jail?"

"He organized a rally with his students at the Miron dumpsite. He was trying to keep the garbage trucks from unloading. It got out of hand, and the police ended up carting everyone away . . ."

Before he can finish the sentence, Arizna, with no warning and for no apparent reason, runs into the neighbouring room. Bemused, Noah wonders what has gotten into her. A minute later, when Arizna returns to the living room and sits down, she seems to have more or less regained her composure.

"Sorry. You were telling me about your thesis director."

"Uh, yes. I don't think he'll stay in jail for very long, but there's no doubt the department will try to have him fired. Holding rallies with students during course hours is not exactly the kind of activity covered by the collective agreement."

"What about you—what are your plans?"

"I'm not sure," Noah answers. "I'm feeling kind of rudderless. I could go back to square one. Buy a trailer and head back to Saskatchewan . . ."

Arizna cuts him off, her forefinger raised like a stop sign. She listens, suddenly stands up and once again disappears into the next room. That's it. Noah is now certain a third party is hiding in the penthouse—an observer, a bodyguard or some kind of accomplice. But an accomplice to what? Then he remembers the story about liberation anthropology that Arizna mentioned the previous summer and, in a flash, pictures a half-dozen guerrillas hidden under the bed.

He gets up, paces, toys with the idea of slipping away. He takes a few steps toward the front door, but then has second thoughts and decides, simply as a matter of courtesy, to tell Arizna goodbye before taking off.

When he walks into the bedroom, Noah is witness to something completely unexpected. On the floor there is a portable cradle, next to a box of disposable diapers and a bag containing medical and pharmaceutical products. Leaning over the bed, Arizna is powdering a baby's bottom with liberal amounts of talcum and softly crooning endearments. She greets Noah's bewildered face with a little smile.

"This is Simón."

She fastens his diaper, buttons his sleeper and, before Noah can object, lays the child in his arms. The archaeologist and the infant observe each other curiously, both of them caught off guard. Noah has trouble seeing Arizna in the role of mother, even though he is holding the evidence in his arms, complete with pink nose, two ears, a tiny penis, a complete set of limbs and a pair of eyes that somehow . . . remind him of . . . someone.

Fourth electric shock of the day: he sees those eyes every morning in the mirror! They are Chipewyan eyes, the soft, skeptical eyes that he inherited from Sarah, who could confirm this on the spot if she were not three thousand kilometres away, somewhere near Calgary.

Noah starts to quake. Disturbed by this, Simón blinks his eyes and wonders whether or not to call for help.

"He's three months old, isn't he?" Noah stammers, after doing the appropriate arithmetic.

"Three months and one week."

"Am I . . . I mean . . . Who's the father?"

"Simón doesn't have a father," Arizna says categorically.

"No father?"

"That's what I said."

Simón starts to cry and flutters his hand in Arizna's direction. She takes him in her arms and, having unbuttoned her blouse, takes out a magnificent, milk-swollen breast. The nipple disappears into the infant's mouth. Eyes wide open, he ravenously gulps down his dose of future.

≈⟩⟨≈

Noah is squeezing the contents of his room into plastic— thirty cubic metres of universe divided into garbage bags whose fate he determines by labelling them *Trash*, *Recycling* or *Salvation Army*, with a felt marker.

He called the people at the research centre to inform them that he would be away "for an indeterminate period of time." While he was on the phone, he asked for news of Thomas Saint-Laurent. All of his students had been set free, but the eminent professor of archaeology would have to cool his heels in jail for another few days. He would in all likelihood be fined for assault, unlawful assembly and obstructing the police, with fifty hours of community volunteer work added on top.

"But the real problem," his secretary whispered, "is that the department will try to get rid of him. Some of his colleagues have wanted his head for years, and they won't miss this chance."

Noah felt it was not the best time to abscond, but, after all, what could a lowly postgraduate student do when a gang of big shots were plotting to lynch each other? Not having any better ideas, he fired off three letters. The first was sent to the student papers in support of Thomas Saint-Laurent. The second went to Thomas Saint-Laurent himself, to assure him of Noah's unconditional moral backing. The third, to Sarah, was intended to let her know that he was once again changing his address.

Everything had happened so quickly that he had barely had time to unpack his bag from Stevenson Island. He washed his clothes in a rush, shook out the layer of lichen at the bottom of the bag, threw out the half-empty bottles of DEET and sunscreen. By harassing civil servants, he managed to secure his passport in forty-eight hours, at an exorbitant price. There was no time for him to get the battery of recommended inoculations, but Arizna— who called the injections "gringo insanities"—told him he could have them administered in Caracas, if it was important to him.

He shoves the plastic bags into a corner and surveys the room with satisfaction. The drawers and shelves are empty, and all that's left to be done is to sweep up so as to leave the room just as he found it five years ago: thirty cubic metres of virgin space. He hooks his pack onto his shoulders, goes out of the room, and closes the door behind him without making any noise.

In the hall he bumps into Maelo, who has had a great vacation, thank you very much.

"How is your Grandmother Úrsula?" Noah inquires.

"She'll bury us all. But what are you up to, with your baggage? Just come back from the North Shore?"

"No, I'm going away."

"Going away?"

"To Venezuela."

"Venezuela?!" Maelo exclaims, in total shock.

"When are you coming back?"

"In about ten years, maybe."

1999

195

The Marvellous Adventures
of Charles Darwin

THE VAST BURGOS FAMILY RESIDENCE was built around 1679, during the same period as the small fort of Santa Rosa. The two buildings, lost in the heights of La Asunción, share the same massive design, meant to withstand the frequent pirate raids to which Margarita Island was subject at the time.

The house is said to have been commissioned by a businessman from Nueva Cádiz, who had made a fortune in the pearl trade and from the enslavement of Guaiquerí Indians. The sudden depletion of the oyster stocks forced him to sell the newly built, never inhabited mansion. Thus hastily disposed of, the troublesome property passed from hand to hand without ever belonging to anyone for very long. It was owned in turn by a general of the Spanish army, a businessman, an architect, five notaries, a member of the National Assembly, a former Brazilian prospector, an English industrialist, a Greek shipowner, and two dentists.

Legend has it that in 1816, during the War of Independence, the mansion was requisitioned for the overnight billeting of Simón Bolívar.

Don Eduardo became the house's fifteenth owner in 1961. He had bought it with the intention of transforming it into a summer home, a rather astonishing idea in light of the building's dimensions. A huge family would be required to occupy the vast patio, the three drawing rooms, the enormous dining room and the ten bedrooms, some furnished with two double beds.

Despite the house's gigantic proportions, no family reunion ever took place there. In fact, it remained practically empty between 1961 and 1995. Don Eduardo's children never came to stay for more than three days a year, and they carefully planned their visits to avoid running into each other. There were no strong bonds among them, and most of them had already absconded to the United States when, in 1976, Arizna's parents died in obscure circumstances off the coast of Trinidad. The assumption was that there had been an explosion on their yacht, but no one was ever able to confirm that hypothesis, least of all Arizna herself, as she was only three years old at the time. She was found the next day, the only survivor, suffering from shock in a half-deflated Zodiac.

This mysterious accident put an end to the family's unbroken presence in South America. Don Eduardo, who was then working at the Venezuelan consulate in

New York, immediately took Arizna under his wing, and began in short order to put all his real estate up for sale, except for the house in La Asunción.

Noah's fascination with this imposing colonial mansion is boundless. Due to his altogether North American naïveté, he believes that Don Eduardo plans to spend his last days on Margarita Island. In fact, the old man rarely turns his thoughts to Venezuela, let alone to the prospect of dying, and has no intention of coming back to live in this house, which he keeps strictly for the arcane tax benefits he derives from it.

At six-thirty on Monday morning, María slips through the small back door, noiselessly crosses the house and, putting the water on to boil, takes command of the kitchen. Hiss of propane, scrape of lighter, clatter of kettle: the music of everyday objects.

The family residence entirely owes its salvation to the presence of this energetic island-dweller who scrubs the floors, dusts the family photos, beats the rugs, scours the dishes, cooks the best *parrilla* on the island, sends overzealous tourists packing and fills the air with her limitless repertoire of Caribbean songs. Without her, this ridiculously large house would in no time sink into gloom and chaos.

Just as she does each morning, she spreads a big red tablecloth over the patio table and sets out plates, preserves and a basketful of bread.

Simón appears around seven o'clock, half-awake, wearing an old Pokémon T-shirt full of holes. María wishes him good morning and combs his hair with a domineering hand. He protests on cue, musses his hair back into its usual tangle and sits down to his bowl of cereal with a yawn.

While María pours him a glass of orange juice, he tilts his nose toward the sky. Not a cloud in sight. A tiny emerald-green hummingbird drones into view, tastes one plant after another as it goes round the patio, then vanishes as swiftly as it appeared. Simón tries to make eye contact with María, seeking in another's wonderment the reflection of his own, but she has gone back to the kitchen, unaware.

Arizna soon comes down, showered, combed and wearing an impeccable suit. She kisses her son on the forehead and sits down with an inaudible sigh of annoyance to the bundle of newspapers just airdropped from Caracas. She pours herself a coffee and starts to peruse the *Meridiano*, turning the pages with a crisp, expert hand. After ten minutes, she checks the time, drains her coffee and goes upstairs for her luggage.

Just as she is leaving the patio, Noah, always last, comes in and shuffles barefoot over to the table. Before he even sits down, Simón breathlessly tells him that a hummingbird no bigger than this (he delineates a microscopic bird) flew in to draw nectar from the banana tree.

"*¿De veras?*" Noah asks, making a show of total amazement.

"Where do the hummingbirds come from?"

"No idea. From the neighbour's garden?"

"*¡No!*" Simón protests. "Do the hummingbirds come from monkeys, like people do?"

Living with a four-and-a-half-year-old allows a person to tap into unsuspected talents. Noah has discovered he has a gift for fabricating nonsensical stories. Last night, when Simón demanded a bedtime story, Noah improvised the first instalment of *The Marvellous Adventures of Charles Darwin on the Galapagos Islands*, an evolutionist tale alive with giant tortoises, fabulous gastropods and "our cousins, the monkeys." Simón's brain has stored away every detail of the story.

Pouring himself a cup of coffee, Noah explains that the hummingbirds are of course descendants of the diplodocus . . .

" . . . and the chicken we ate last night was the great-great-great-grandson of a *Tyrannosaurus rex*."

Simón bursts out laughing. He likes this peculiar genealogy. Now he needs to be provided with some books on the subject. As he chews, Noah wonders if somewhere on this planet there might be a publisher who has thought of putting out a children's book on dinosaurs and hummingbirds. It won't be long before Simón learns to read, and Noah has no intention of letting him decipher his first words from an old road map.

Arizna returns to the patio with a frown, her flight bag slung over her shoulder, already looking exhausted even though the day has hardly begun. The truth is that despite a difficult start—and thanks to the financial backing of Don Eduardo—the Tortuga publishing house has become a going concern, such that Arizna's responsibilities have grown tenfold. She is now director and public relations officer for Editorial Tortuga, editor-in-chief of the *El Pututo* quarterly, conference organizer, researcher and lecturer at the Instituto Indigenista Autónomo—positions that involve travelling to Ecuador, Bolivia and Peru for meetings with other researchers of indigenous peoples. She is also writing a manuscript on the history of Aboriginal women in South America from 1492 to 1992, in her spare time.

She crosses the patio, leans down to Simón and whispers something in his ear. The child smiles and nods his head while hollowing out little craters in his cereal. Arizna kisses him and goes toward the main door. Noah accompanies her, coffee in hand.

"When are you due back, exactly?"

"Tomorrow night. If you need to, you can always call me on my cell."

She walks through the garden, pushes open the gate and steps out onto the sidewalk. She flags a passing cab with a regal wave. Squeal of tires and rattle of rusted metal. Arizna leans into the window and negotiates the run to the airport. The driver feigns indignation, on cue, before making a little sign of agreement with his hand. Arizna opens the door, throws her bag inside and points a mock-tyrannical finger at Noah.

"You take good care of Simón!"

Noah bows in comic reverence. The next moment, the taxi fades away in a billow of smoking oil.

The Distressing Saga of the Garifunas

THE NOTION OF PATERNITY has always been an elusive one. Unlike maternity, which is legitimated de facto by the spectacular nature of pregnancy, paternity is difficult to put one's finger on. No eyewitness can be called to testify on the genitor's behalf, no birthing can prove his blood ties with the child. The status of father did not truly come into its own until the introduction of DNA tests, an ultimately inglorious consecration since, in resorting to this, shall we say, legal procedure, the genitor admits his inability to have his status acknowledged through traditional diplomacy. In making public the test results, he establishes his biological paternity but thereupon sacrifices his social paternity.

That is the reason why Noah never tried to lay claim to the title of Simón's father. He would have preferred a simple avowal from Arizna to the crass materialism of DNA. But in the face of his many queries on the subject, she steadfastly denied, contested and refuted any involvement of a Chipewyan gamete in the conception of her little boy. "Simón is 100 per cent Venezuelan," she affirmed. The child's eyes forcefully contradicted this assertion, but Noah chose not to press the point. Arizna jealously protected this strange independence of hers, and he was bound to respect it, at least insofar as he wished to avoid being deported to some far-off Aleutian island. One day Simón would be in a position to understand certain things—in particular, that despite its complex workings, the machinery of sex remains the simplest aspect of that great piece of handiwork so pompously referred to as Our Civilization.

In the meantime, Noah preferred to piece together a small, quotidian paternity comprised of knowing winks and smiles, lazy breakfasts, and days at the beach. To do this he had to stay on Margarita Island, and to stay there he needed a pretext, a complicated pretext if at all possible, with numerous detours and dead ends, so as to fend off questions.

He remembered an article he had read several years before, in an old *National Geographic* that he'd found behind the refrigerator while cleaning up. He discovered in that article a story so complicated as to be perfectly suited to the circumstances, a story that could have been titled:

THE DISTRESSING SAGA OF THE GARIFUNAS

It all began in the year of grace 1635, when a Dutch slaver, sailing in from Africa with its human cargo, ran aground in the Grenadine archipelago.

The slaves took advantage of the mayhem to wipe out the ship's crew and escape. They found refuge on the nearby island of Yurumein (subsequently renamed St. Vincent) and threw their lot in with the Caribs. The tribes stemming from this intermingling, neither wholly Amerindian nor entirely African, soon took on the name of Garifuna, although, depending on the circumstances, the location, and the subtleties of the prevailing grammar, they were also known as Garinagu, Carifuna, Kalypuna, Garif, Karif, Caberne, Cabre, Calino, Calinya, Calinyaku or Callinago, these being nothing more than an ongoing deformation of the name Carib.

The Maroons of St. Lucia and Barbados soon joined the Garifunas, drawn by the prospect of living in freedom on this island that was still unoccupied by Europeans. But it was a tenuous freedom, for ever since the massacres of St. Kitts in 1626, the French and British had been embroiled in an intense rivalry over control of the archipelago. During the next two centuries, the Lesser Antilles became the theatre of countless battles, associations, betrayals, invasions, uprisings, treaties, edicts and other more or less diplomatic altercations.

The Garifunas would surely have remained on the

periphery of this conflict if not for the signing of the Treaty of Paris in 1763.

When France ceded the island of St. Vincent to the British, it placed the islanders in a delicate position, especially the Garifunas, whose ambiguous historical situation must not be forgotten: neither wholly Aboriginal nor entirely descended from the African slaves.

Political uncertainty put revolt back on the order of the day.

The Garifunas wanted to expel the British from the island, and to this end they made the mistake of allying themselves with the French. For its part, France, which had never been weaker, had been reduced to fomenting insurrections among the local populations as an inexpensive method of driving out the British. The manoeuvre turned out to be futile since, in the absence of solid French bases elsewhere in the archipelago, each island won in this way would subsequently be returned to Great Britain under the next treaty.

The last insurrections took place in February 1795, when the French attempted simultaneous landings in Grenada, St. Lucia and St. Vincent. The results were disastrous, and by 1796 only the Garifunas continued to resist. British troops overran the island and succeeded in crushing the rebellion in St. Vincent, thus putting an end to two hundred years of war in the Caribbean.

In January 1797, the administration of St. Vincent ordered the deportation of the insurgents. The operation was carried out with devastating efficiency—Acadia had clearly provided the British with a prodigious training ground. They burned the pirogues and the crops, and more than four thousand islanders found themselves crammed into a processing station on the minuscule island of Baliceaux, where they were left to starve for a month. The survivors were then classed according to skin colour. The fairest were sent to St. Vincent (where cheap labour had suddenly become scarce), while those with darker complexions—that is, the Garifunas—were once again herded into the holds of ships and deported.

On the night of April 12, 1797, after several weeks at sea, they were abandoned on Roatán Island, off the coast of Honduras.

Enfeebled by their living conditions over the recent months, the deportees were bound to die of exhaustion, mosquito attacks or the onslaught of the Spanish colonists. That, at any rate, was what the British believed. Against all odds, they survived, crossed the continent and spread out from Nicaragua to the British Honduras. Two centuries later, the Garifunas still inhabit Central America. They continue to fish, cook cassava, speak their ancestral language, and mistrust the spirits haunting the river mouths, where the fresh water and the salt water mingle.

And no one, not even the greatest ethnologists, can properly explain the intricate mechanism that allowed these orphans, though uprooted and exiled, to hold on to their identity.

Noah's life on this island essentially boils down to telling stories. At night he invents evolutionary fables about Charles Darwin, while during the day he claims that the reason he is in Margarita is to write a doctoral dissertation on the Garifunas.

209

To the inquisitive, he states that he is interested in the relationship between the Garifunas' oral tradition and the colonial archives. And, he asserts, many early archival holdings have remained on Margarita Island, more precisely at the National Archives of La Asunción, barely a ten-minute walk from the Burgos residence, which, fundamentally, provides him with an ideal pretext to live under the same roof as Simón.

Arizna has taken the bait. She precisely remembers their first discussion on the fifth floor of the university library in Montreal, and it makes perfect sense to her that Noah would be interested in issues of relocation, traditional territories and identity. She has even asked him several times to write an article on the Garifunas for *El Pututo*, but each time he has cleverly managed to push back the deadline.

He has developed a genuine talent for storytelling.

So long as a bona fide Garifunas expert does not alight on Margarita and unmask Noah, he can enjoy life to the fullest. He pretends to study, earns a little money teaching English and French, basks in the sun. And whenever he has the chance, he takes Simón to the beach.

Keratin

HALF-PAST MIDNIGHT. In the space between the sky-scrapers, clementine-coloured patches of cloud drift by. A few snowflakes flutter through the air. The atmosphere is that of a Japanese animated film, five minutes before the end of the world.

Joyce adjusts her scarf. Standing in the entrance to an underground parking lot, she feels strangely indifferent as she observes the scene bathed in a yellowish light. This garage is truly an Ali Baba's cave, with its inadequate surveillance, plentiful trash bins and the treasures that can often be found here. Tonight, however, all she sees is an icy crypt that reeks of concrete and motor oil.

This sudden lack of interest leaves her perplexed. Is it a sign that she should consider retiring? She looks at her watch. The last Metro leaves in ten minutes. She could go back home, take a hot bath, empty her bottle of rum—and just forget about the memory of Herménégilde Doucette.

Two blocks south, a police siren can be heard wailing down the street. Joyce shrugs and walks into the parking garage.

No sign of life. Here and there, a few vehicles have been left behind, surrounded by puddles of oil and litter. The car owners must be doing overtime, twelve floors up.

Joyce glances scornfully at the surveillance cameras. She knows how to go unnoticed. She edges along the walls, cuts over to the third pillar, crosses the garage following a specific angle, skirts another section of wall and ends up directly in front of the dumpsters.

She opens the first one and shines her flashlight inside.

A face appears in the beam.

Joyce stops herself from recoiling. She quickly regains her poise and proceeds to examine the situation with a cool head.

A woman is lying among the garbage bags—most likely an employee tossed out due to downsizing. Under the sensible beige suit, her body has become perfectly mummified. The limbs have atrophied and the skin has taken on the shiny tautness of smoked herring. With her arms crossed over her chest and a tense smile, she waits for the garbage to be collected with the serenity of an Egyptian queen.

How long has she been there? Joyce takes a whiff. No noticeable odour. She presses the tip of her forefinger against the corpse. As light as papier mâché.

In the course of her nocturnal outings, Joyce has come across many oddities, but nothing remotely like this. She sweeps her flashlight over the body from head to foot, fascinated by its angularity, its empty eye sockets. She has the impression of looking at a distorted mirror image of herself.

Then she comes back to earth. Best not to hang around.

Just as she is about to lower the lid, she notices an ID card pinned to the mummy's blouse. Under the black-and-white photo, an ordinary employee: Susie Legault / No. 3445.

Joyce carefully removes the card and slips it into her coat pocket. Then she closes the container ever so gently, as if afraid of waking the mummy.

The incredibly cluttered state of the apartment would suggest that an insane hostage-taker has just spent three days holed up within these walls. But there is no one here, no one but Joyce, and she has assumed the roles of both captor and hostage.

No sooner had she returned from the centre of town than she took refuge under her work lamp, with a bottle of rum on the port side and the tools of her trade to starboard. It is nearly six in the morning, yet so much remains to be done.

She pulls an identity card from her pocket and examines it carefully. Then, with three strokes of a razor blade, she shucks the plastic sleeve and excises the photo. She glues her own in the blank space, deftly forges the expiration date and slides the whole thing into the lamination machine. The smell of melted vinyl instantly floods the room—the aroma typical of a change of identity. The machine spits out the card, hot and glistening like keratin.

Voilà! Joyce's name from now on will be Susie Legault.

A shiver runs through her as she examines her new skin. She thinks back to the woman lying amid the trash, her bones jutting out under her business suit.

From a shelf, she takes down a shoebox stuffed with IDs recycled from the rubbish: baptismal records, certificates of civil status, student cards, magnetic or bar-code passes, library cards, video-club membership cards, ISIC cards, health insurance cards and even a quite credible passport. The same picture is repeated dozens of times, always hastily taken in the automatic booth at the Berri-UQAM Metro station, a cheap portrait of a nice young girl auditioning for a lookalike contest.

Joyce nonchalantly adds her new card to the collection.

She rubs her eyes, swollen from lack of sleep, unplugs the laminator and pushes the work lamp away from her eyes. The light falls on Leslie Lynn Doucette.

The newspaper clippings, always pinned up in the same spot, have turned a shade of amber.

Joyce has combed the Internet repeatedly, looking for the missing link that might elucidate the ties between her and this distant cousin. But what she has learned from her research amounts to nothing more useful than Michael Doucet's prolific contribution to the Cajun group Beausoleil, the address of Elvis Doucette Muffler Service (4500 Road 67, Lafayette, Louisiana) and the existence of Neimann-Pick type D disease, a hereditary condition widespread among the Acadian community of Yarmouth County in southern Nova Scotia, which has been traced back to the seventeenth century and is attributable to marriages between blood relations.

Even the massive genealogical archives of the Mormons are of no help in untangling the branches of her family tree. Nothing on Leslie Lynn Doucette, or Herménégilde Doucette, or the family's buccaneering vocation. Grandfather Lyzandre apparently knew something the genealogists did not.

She still has to download tonight's email. With a finger-flick she wakes up Louis-Olivier Gamache, fifty-seventh avatar of the species, and logs on to the Internet. A minute later, Eudora announces: 96 new messages.

None of these messages is addressed to her. In the last ten years she has not received a single email in her name. Not one *Dear Joyce*, or *Dear Miss Doucette*, or

Hi, Jo! Piracy demands absolute anonymity, and Joyce has always hidden behind one or another of the false identities fished out of the garbage.

In a single glance, she spots and annihilates the spam—email publicity spawned by super-robots equipped with a business dictionary, a grammar corrector and a copy of *How to Win Friends and Influence People*, capable of firing off ten thousand new messages per minute: *Want to earn more money? Stop Hair Loss Now! Lose 30 Pounds in 30 Days, Guaranteed! Increased Sexual Potency! Hot Casino Action—Try for Free! Brand New—Just Launched—Be the First!*

That leaves the business correspondence, written in a vast variety of languages: the ornate slang of the Cayman Islands, the telegraphic Spanish of Mexico, the elliptical Japanese of Osaka. Not to mention the picturesque Anglo-Russian of a certain Dimitri, a seventeen-year-old Muscovite hacker sustained by little more than Brezhnev Cola.

She glumly observes the stream of credit card numbers, IP addresses and fragments of source code.

For the second time tonight, Joyce experiences a deep-seated weariness. The little universe of piracy is exhausting. Information spills out on every side, circulates at lightning speed and almost instantly fades into obsolescence. The moment you slow down you are left behind, so that life soon turns into an endless series of expiration dates.

Joyce looks at her watch. In three hours she must report for work at the fish store.

She yawns and looks outside. The sky is gradually growing blue over Montreal. For a brief instant, she has the impression of looking not through a window but at another cathode screen.

She presses her nose against the glass and peers at the old building across the street. Curtains are drawn back. One family after another is waking up.

In the tiny window of a bathroom, a man is shaving and cautiously pushes his nose up out of the way with his forefinger. A couple of windows farther along, a woman is making breakfast while a long-haired young girl hastily does her math homework on the edge of the table.

Joyce feels she is living on the outskirts of a precious world that is slipping away. On the other side of this window, events take their course and there is no stopping them, no way of affecting their inherent logic. Each second, each moment, unfolds for the first and last time. The process cannot be interrupted, cannot be reversed, cannot be copied or backed up.

The windowpane has misted over from Joyce's breath. The outside world gradually recedes, and reality seems more and more a relative thing. She wipes the window with her sleeve. On the other side of the street, the long-haired girl has finished her math homework and is putting her notebooks away in a brightly coloured backpack.

Joyce starts to shiver, even though it's warm in the apartment. She turns to the computer hoping to find something to latch on to, a certainty, but the spell has been broken. On the screen, the words are no longer meant for her. The objects around her seem foreign. It is as if she has awoken from a long dream and finds herself sitting at someone else's desk.

Looking around, she discovers only one object that is familiar to her: the photograph of Susie Legault, employee No. 3445, abandoned in a wastebasket.

Little by little, the odour of melted vinyl fades away.

María Libre

NOAH AND SIMÓN, with sandals on their feet and towels around their necks, burst out of the house running. Just as they are leaving the garden, they collide with the mailman. After a moment of disarray, the old man straightens his cap and glasses, before handing an envelope to Noah.

It's a letter for Sarah, addressed to General Delivery in Relay and returned with the notice: *No Such Post Office.*

Noah shrugs and dashes off again. Simón, who is still a good ten metres ahead, shouts for him to *Come on!* and *Hurry up!* At the corner of the street, they jump on the old sky-blue bus that goes down to Juangriego.

As it leaves La Asunción, the bus route crosses the flight corridor of the Santiago Mariño airport. A roar fills the air, and Simón thrusts his head out the window just in time to see the white belly of a Boeing brush over the hillside in slow motion. The airplane gains altitude, veers off toward the mainland and dissolves into the sun, while the crowded blue bus continues on its way down to the seashore in a thundering racket of steel.

The simple pleasures of a bus ride.

Waves of dust and pollen blow in through the windows. The driver steers his vehicle lackadaisically, fiddling with the radio buttons all the while. Amid the crackling, the tuner pulls in a few measures of *cumbia* and fragments of detergent commercials. Three times in every kilometre, the bus must take on or drop off a passenger. At each stop, the brakes groan as if about to commit their souls to God in the next few metres. And when they move off again, it's the transmission's turn to utter its death rattle. Between these two threats, the bus rolls along without much trouble, aided—it should be said—by the slope.

After an endless series of hairpin curves, the road comes out at sea level and shoots straight toward the water. Each time, Noah hopes the bus will not stop, but keep on sailing over the water toward the horizon.

After the exit to Juangriego, the houses are more dispersed. The roadside is filled with watercraft, fishing gear, rickety shacks and then, finally, there you are at the María Libre beach. Screech of brakes, groan of transmission—Noah and Simón find themselves alone before the ocean's immensity.

Simón dashes across the road and through the stand of coconut trees, swoops over the beach sloughing his clothes off behind him and plunges naked, headlong, into the surf.

Noah grins and unrolls the bamboo mat in the exact middle of the beach, where he can easily supervise the boy. He is fascinated by the tremendous amount of energy that radiates from this little *Homo sapiens*. Every minute, he leaps out of the water holding a new treasure: gold coin, emerald, ivory figurine. Noah greets the artifacts with cheerful shouts and jams them into an old plastic bag, their improvised strongbox, which is soon overflowing with dripping stones, shards of polished glass, and shells that here and there are shaken up by hermit crabs trying to break free.

Noah had never set foot on a beach before coming to Margarita Island, and this belated discovery has overwhelmed him. Gazing at the sea, he once again experiences the dizziness one feels on the great plains of Saskatchewan. The monotone roar of the waves is reminiscent of the wind in the barley fields, and triggers a state of mind conducive to the fabrication of crazy stories that he will tell Simón that night.

The setting would be perfect if not for the presence of the *Granma*, an old yacht abandoned by the side of the road years ago, whose condition is in constant decline. The portholes have been smashed, the hull is falling apart under layers of rust. Half peeled away on the lower stern, the ship's name (*La Granma*) and its home port (*Tuxpan-Mexico*) can be made out. Perched on a makeshift cradle, it resembles a grim wading bird lurking among the coconut trees.

Noah eyes the *Granma* warily and with a peculiar uneasiness. The old yacht reminds him of boat people, and he cannot help but imagine the family of Cuban refugees who once found themselves drifting off Miami Beach in this dilapidated old tub. He wonders what his life might have looked like had he grown up on a boat rather than in a trailer.

Late in the afternoon, on the far side of the bay, the sun goes down suddenly and without warning.

Shielding his eyes with his hand, Noah observes the sky. Off the coast of Trinidad the horizon has turned suspiciously opaque. High above the territorial waters, a great mass of rain is gathering. For now, though, only the precursory cirrus clouds are visible, those fine particles of ice floating ten thousand metres above sea level.

Noah removes his shirt and dives in to retrieve Simón, who threatens to grow gills and never leave the ocean again. With teasing carelessness, he hoists the little rebel on his shoulder, carries him back to dry land and, over the boy's protests, gives him a vigorous rubdown with his towel. The same scene is repeated every time they go to the beach. Simón seems to be a prototype for a new human subspecies, half-terrestrial, half-aquatic. But might this not be just the normal demeanour of an island-dweller?

They get dressed, try in vain to shake the sand out of their clothes and, while scarfing down the chorizo sandwiches that María made for them, run to catch the old sky-blue bus going back up to La Asunción.

As they approach the road, Noah turns to take a last look at the stand of coconut trees. The *Granma*, alone and ominous on its stilts, seems to be watching them.

Colonial Archives

On both sides of the road, a cornfield goes on forever, as vast as the Pacific Ocean. Nothing interrupts
the horizontal perfection of the immense plain.
Nothing except, to the southwest, a tiny silhouette.

At first it resembles an elephant propped up on
crutches and saddled with a pagoda. The silhouette
gradually grows larger, more distinct, until finally
it's the *Granma* that comes into view, crossing the
prairie on iron stilts, straight out of Salvador Dalí's
surrealist menagerie. It advances diagonally, indifferent to the layout of the fields, cutting a wide swath
through the corn. With each huge stride, long metallic groans ring out, and large flakes of rust drop away
from the hull.

It crosses Route 627 and disappears heading north-
northwest.

Noah sits up in his bed, eyes wide open.

He wipes the sweat from his forehead.

The clock says five in the morning, and the room temperature is close to 30 degrees Celsius. There's no point in trying to go back to sleep now.

He turns on the bedside lamp, grumbling as he rubs his eyes. He looks for a book on the night table, but all he finds is the dog-eared copy of *Moby-Dick* that Arizna lent him. He has made several attempts at reading this daunting book, all in vain; Herman Melville bores him. Come to think of it, wouldn't that be the best way to go back to sleep? The book opens of its own accord at chapter 44. Noah skims a few paragraphs, but the oppressive presence of the *Granma* still weighs heavily on his chest.

He gets up noiselessly and goes out into the corridor.

In the adjoining room, Simón is fast asleep, arms and legs spread out like a little starfish. Standing in the doorway, Noah muses over the child's slumber, flawless and untroubled by phantoms.

He shuts the door and goes down to wait for sunrise on the patio.

After four years of exile on Margarita Island, Noah has made friends with only one person: Bernardo Báez, superintendent, secretary, treasurer and director of the colonial archives of La Asunción—archives that amount to no more than a few dozen boxes crammed inside a forgotten cubbyhole of city hall.

When he was a teenager, Bernardo had a Great Dream. He would become an expert in marine archaeology and go live on the Mediterranean coast. Every night, immersed in the turquoise waters of his obsession, he discovered Phoenician shipwrecks, Alexandrine sphinxes, submerged amphorae. In 1993 he went to study history in Caracas, the first leg of a centrifugal voyage that, in theory, was to take him farther and farther from his native island.

He enjoyed two years of freedom in the capital, until his father was drowned in a fishing accident. Bernardo returned home for the funeral and decided to stay for several weeks to help his mother, who adamantly refused to leave Margarita. The arrangement was supposed to be only temporary. It went from temporary to transitional, from transitional to permanent, and now, four years later, Bernardo is still mired in the daily routine of the sun-drenched island. He works half-heartedly in the colonial archives, a poorly paid sinecure barely a step up from hawking seashell necklaces to tourists. No one ever comes to consult the archives aside from old Javier Salazar Ramirez, a silent, hundred-year-old genealogist who every other day gets locked in after closing hours.

Needless to say, Bernardo welcomes Noah each morning like a saviour.

The two companions roll up their sleeves, sit down at the enormous writing table and play checkers. From opening to closing time, they pass the hours lazily moving the pieces, drinking oversweet instant coffee and discussing marine archaeology, Venezuelan politics and the local gossip. Noah corrects Bernardo's French, and he in turn corrects Noah's Spanish.

Bernardo is the only person on the island who knows the truth about Noah, and this knowledge obliges him to refute the countless rumours going around. Whenever questioned, he assures the questioner that Noah is toiling day and night toward his doctorate on the Garifunas. Friendship is sometimes more important than truth.

When Noah confided in him, Bernardo had a good laugh: "If people only knew what the archives *really* contain!" he said. For in fact, most of the interesting documents had been reduced to ashes in 1816, during the War of Independence. Nothing remains now of the original archives but bundles of genealogical records interspersed with documents pertaining to church foundations, anonymous shipwrecks, and land registers, all mixed up in some thirty cardboard boxes, which on very humid days give off an overpowering odour of smoke.

It is precisely this sooty stench that hangs in the room when, at nine a.m. sharp, Noah and Simón walk through the doors of the archives.

Simón comes in first, looking rather pleased to be there, although, after serious consideration, a day at the archives is no match for a day at the beach. He crosses the room rubbing his hands together, opens one of the cabinets with the self-assurance of a regular visitor, and takes out a handful of coloured pencils and a sheaf of white paper. Then, satisfied that he is reasonably well supplied, he sits down at the end of the table

and begins to draw.

At this point Noah shuffles in, obviously lacking sleep. He pauses in the doorway and sniffs the air.

"Sure looks like it's going to rain," he mutters.

"Don't you read the papers?" Bernardo answers, as he steps out of the washroom holding a copy of *Últimas Noticias*. "They're predicting storms all week."

"*Carajo*," Noah complains after an extended yawn. "It reeks of old charcoal."

Then he lifts his nose again and changes his mind.

"Hey, doesn't it also smell of instant coffee?"

"Can I serve you a double, very sweet?"

"Well, if you insist."

While Bernardo is fixing the vile beverage, Noah watches Simón working away with his pencils. On the next table, the checkerboard and pieces have been laid out, announcing an apparently normal day. At the far end of the room, Javier Salazar Ramirez is huffing like a furnace as he pores over a bulky register. He seems not to have left his chair for days, and Noah wonders if he again spent the night in the archives.

"So, *muchacho!*" Bernardo says as he hands him the steaming cup. "Ready to lose your first game of the day?"

Noah shrugs indifferently.

"You don't seem to be in very good shape," says Bernardo, as he places the checkers on the board.

"Insomnia."

"More nightmares?"

"The *Granma* again."

Bernardo gestures to him to start the game. Noah takes a sip of coffee, sits down and distractedly makes the first move. Bernardo counterattacks in the opposite corner.

"So, Arizna has gone to Caracas?"

"How did you guess?"

"Because of the nightmares."

Noah's index finger freezes on the checker he is about to move.

"Excuse me?"

"Haven't you noticed," Bernardo explains, without raising his eyes from the checkerboard, "that the only time you dream about the *Granma* is when Arizna is away?"

For a moment, Noah searches for an answer that would cut short this line of questioning. But there's nothing to be said—Bernardo is right.

"How is your mother?" he finally asks as he moves his checker.

"Fine, thanks, and yours?"

"I wouldn't know."

"Where is she, these days?"

"Somewhere near Medicine Hat, I guess. We always spent December in southern Alberta."

At the back of the room, the genealogist laboriously turns the pages of the register. The procedure raises so much dust that the old man occasionally disappears behind a cloud, and might be thought to have disappeared altogether if not for his constant coughing and snorting. Bernardo casts an annoyed glance in his direction before moving a checker, muttering under his breath.

"What is he up to, exactly?" Noah asks. "For years now, I've watched him sifting through the same papers."

"Don Javier? He's half out of his mind. He's got all kinds of theories about marriages, births . . . *la herencia?*"

"Heredity."

"*Lo que sea*. He believes that if you unite all the families of Margarita in a single family tree, you can predict the future of the island."

"I see."

The cloud of dust grows larger around the old man and turns into a veritable cumulonimbus. Evidently the omens in the old registers are not at all favourable. Noah gives Simón a protective look. The boy has slapped a sheet of paper down on the table and, armed with a grey felt pen, is reproducing the Great Hurricane of 1780.

"Are you planning on going back to Caracas soon?" Noah asks.

Bernardo hesitates. He studies his opponent's last move, which jeopardizes the western flank of the board.

"Don't know. Next year, maybe."

"You said that last year."

"Nothing is simple where my mother is concerned. Whenever I make plans to leave, she threatens to get sick. Or she asks me to stay one more year. Or she goes on a hunger strike. Or she tries to marry me off to Gladis, the neighbour's daughter."

There's an awkward pause. Bernardo offhandedly captures one of Noah's checkers.

"The truth is, I should have gone back to Caracas right after my father's funeral. Now, the situation is becoming more and more complicated. I won't be able to leave so long as my mother is alive, and she is sure to live to one hundred. And if this goes on, I'm going to end up wishing for her to die."

He looks up from the checkerboard, horrified at having said these last words aloud. His gaze falls on Don Javier, still immersed in his register.

"I hope to leave before I reach that point," he murmurs.

Noah wonders if Bernardo meant "leave before wishing for my mother's death" or "leave before I look like Don Javier" or "leave before Don Javier's genealogical predictions turn out to be right." But he chooses not to add anything more, and the rest of the game takes place in an embarrassed silence.

An hour later, as Noah and Simón leave the colonial archives with bundles of drawings rolled up under their arms, the first drops of rain have started to come down.

All Directions at Once

~

IT HAS BEEN RAINING FOR THREE DAYS NOW. Ever since this morning, I've been hoping for the incursion of some unusual customer: an armed Sandinista, Bluebeard or simply a second-hand bookstore robber. But no one has come through the door as yet, and I've spent the whole day wrapped up in my dreams and an old woollen blanket.

I stretch and blink at the clock. Five to five. I decide to close right away, and to hell with convention. Just as I'm about to get up, the little doorbell jingles, and for a brief instant the door opens onto the storm. As soon as the mist clears, I recognize my favourite book thief, dressed in a raincoat with blackened seams and a pair of jeans soaked to mid-thigh.

She greets me with a nod, drops her sailor's bag on the doormat and, before I can say a word, vanishes between two sections.

The whole scene plays out so quickly that, without the sailor's duffel and the puddle spreading around it,

I would think I was dreaming. I rub my eyes and look out the display window. No bookseller in his right mind would do overtime in this miserable weather. I slip out of my blanket and go over to the cookbook section. The girl is not there. I crane my neck toward the computer section. Not there either. I scratch my head. Something in the universe is awry.

I find the girl at the back of the bookstore, near the washroom, in front of the travel section. While trying not to rush her, I ask her if she needs any help. She thanks me nonchalantly and lets me know she can manage on her own.

"It's almost five o'clock. I'm going to have to close up."

"Oh?" she says, looking at her watch. "I didn't notice how fast time was passing."

"No problem. Have you found what you were looking for?"

"Not really. I'm looking for a travel guide."

I wait for her to specify a country—the Fiji Islands, Japan, Madagascar but she adds nothing else. The sentence ends right there, abruptly, as if the destination were of minor importance. I let this pass and behave as though it were perfectly normal for someone to want to buy just any guide, in preparation for a trip to just anywhere.

Unfortunately, I explain to her, our bookstore is rather poorly stocked in travel guides, whatever the destination might be. We do, of course, have a travel section—one can't do without—but, to be perfectly honest, I snap up most of the guides as they come into the store. We all have our little obsessions.

The girl looks put out. Undaunted, I offer to lend her a guide from my personal collection. (I subtly stress the word *lend*, but she does not react.)

"I'm going away very soon," she replies, after a brief moment of hesitation. "I won't have time to return it to you."

"Well then, take it with you. Books have to travel. You can give it back to me when you come back, or you can send it back to me in the mail, covered with exotic stamps."

"I don't know . . . I wouldn't want you to go to any trouble."

"No, I insist! Just tell me what sort of guide you're looking for. I'll bring a dozen of them tomorrow morning and all you have to do is come by and make your choice. How does that sound?"

"Tomorrow will be too late. Do you think we could meet later tonight?"

This catches me off guard. I agree and scribble my address on the back of a bookstore business card.

"It's in Little Italy, right opposite Dante Park . . ."

"I know the neighbourhood. Say around seven?"

I nod yes. She smiles as she slips the card in her pocket and, without saying anything more, heads toward the door. Just as she is about to leave, I come to my senses and ask her name.

"Joyce," she answers, after wavering for a split second.

The next moment she disappears into the cyclone. Rooted by the door, I stare at the bell dancing in mid-air. The clock shows 5:03 p.m. I do a little jig and set about closing the shop. There are no receipts to total up—an advantage of the days when there are no sales—so all I need to do is camouflage the cash-register drawer in its usual hiding place, behind the ten-volume *Encyclopaedia of Maritime Disasters*.

Outside, St-Laurent Boulevard has vanished beneath a dun-coloured downpour. Anything lying on the ground is mercilessly borne away toward the river: newspapers, gloves and tuques, fast-food wrappers, crumpled plastic bags bobbing on the current with jellyfish throbs. Not a car in sight, no one on the sidewalks.

A foretaste of the end of the world.

When I arrive home, I look like a drowned man who's just been dragged from a lake by the Sûreté du Québec. I remove my shoes, hastily wring out my socks, and cross the living room without turning on the lights. Somewhere in the shadows, I trip on the grating of the hot-air vent that I've been planning to screw back down for two months. I wrench my ankle and crash to the floor. The grating slides across the wood floor, ricochets with a clang and disappears into the darkness.

Right then, someone knocks at the door. I limp over to open it.

It's Joyce, an hour ahead of time. She drops her old sailor's duffel in the hallway and, shivering, hangs up her raincoat.

"Am I too early?"

"Not at all," I say, rubbing my little toe. "You look like you've just rounded Cape Horn in a cardboard box. Can I get you a dry sweater?"

"No, thanks."

"A hot drink, then?"

"That would be nice."

I hobble over to the kitchen. While I'm putting on the kettle, Joyce tosses her boots in a corner of the hallway and ventures into the living room.

"Watch your step—there's a hole in the floor."

The warning is wasted. She's found the switch. Out of the darkness come sea serpents and horned whales with torrents of water spewing out of their nostrils.

Amused, Joyce contemplates the facsimile of a nautical map dated 1675, the margins decorated with compass roses and legendary monsters. She adjusts her glasses and steps closer to the map, evidently intrigued by the environs of Hispaniola Island. I spy on her as I measure out the tea leaves.

How strange it is to see this girl in my living room. I know nothing about her, really, except for her tendency to steal computer-programming handbooks. She seems harmless enough, with her little reading glasses and her short hair, but for all I know she could be a dangerous outlaw on the run. Tired of petty thievery, she may have knocked off six banks in a row. In which case, her old sailor's duffel probably contains a gun as long as a harpoon, and a sheaf of blood-soaked banknotes.

I can almost hear the sound of gunfire, but then a high-pitched whistle interrupts my flight of fancy. Shaking my head, I take the kettle off the stove and crane my neck toward the living room. "The travel guides are in the small bookcase, behind you."

When I step out of the kitchen with a steaming teapot of oolong, Joyce is perusing my travel guides.

"You've travelled a lot," she says, without taking her eyes off the bookcase.

"Me? Never set foot outside Montreal. My longest trip was when I left Châteauguay."

"So why all these guides?"

"My mother collected them. After she died, I kept up the collection."

"Your mother liked to travel?"

"No. It's quite odd, actually, because she worked in a travel agency. She could have gone around the world for free, but she preferred to spend the summer in the backyard with her feet in the plastic wading pool and a pile of books at her side. Ultimately, I think she liked travel guides better than travelling."

I pour the tea through a cloud of steam. Joyce takes the cup between her hands to warm herself and sits down on the couch cross-legged. "Tea . . . ," she murmurs as she sniffs her cup. Immediately, a peculiar tautness seems to flow out of her body. She suddenly appears exhausted, slightly stooped and with dark rings under her eyes.

"When I was small, I would go see my grandfather every day after school. He had a Ming dynasty teapot, blue and white porcelain, with a long crack running through it, and completely red on the inside. We drank bitter tea, and he would tell me pirate stories."

She yawns. There's a pause. Her eyes grow smaller and smaller, swollen with fatigue.

"What sort of pirates?" I ask, by way of prompting her to continue.

"All kinds. I think he'd learned his stories from an old sailor's almanac. But he talked mainly about our ancestors. It seems my great-great-great-grandfather was a renowned Acadian pirate. I was never able to verify that. He talked so much about it that I ended up wanting to become a pirate. My cousins said women pirates didn't exist, but the more often they said it, the more I wanted to prove them wrong. Sometimes kids get strange notions into their heads."

"Not at all. As a matter of fact, women pirates did exist. There were two of them among the crew of Calico Rackham."

"Red Rackham?!" she exclaims in a burst of laughter. "Aren't you getting that mixed up with a Tintin story?"

"Hergé always drew on true stories. The real Red Rackham lived in the Bahamas in the eighteenth century. His name was Jack Rackham, but he was nicknamed Calico Rackham. He had a pretty run-of-the-mill career, and the English hanged him after a few years."

She perks up, visibly revived by the discussion.

"My grandfather never told me about him. Who were the two women?"

"I've forgotten their names. One of them was called Bonny something."

"Bonnie Parker?" she jokes.

"I can't remember. But they're relatively well known. Legend has it they were the only ones to defend the ship when the English broadsided them. The rest of the crew were dead drunk and cowering below deck."

"How romantic!"

"I've got a book on the subject, if you're interested."

I have an exact picture of the book in my head. It's the Three-Headed Book, forgotten by a customer at the bookshop in 1994.

As I walk over to the bookcase, I realize I haven't laid eyes on that book for quite some time. I quickly locate a number of books without covers—I like books that have had a rough time of it. I grab the first one, but it's only a threadbare copy of the *Ashley Book of Knots*. With the second book I'm sure my luck has turned, but it's the 1945 edition of Damase Potvin's *Saint-Laurent et ses îles*. The third is an inexpensive copy of *Robinson Crusoe*, and the fourth a fragment of *Japan Expedition* by Matthew Perry.

After going through my entire library, I have to face the fact: I've lost a book, an extraordinary delinquency that makes me the disgrace of the Guild of Booksellers. I resign myself to consulting an ordinary travel guide on the Bahamas.

"Have you found it?" Joyce asks, pouring herself more tea.

"No," I reply, blushing. "But as Jack Rackham was based on Providence Island, there should be some mention of him in the history of the Bahamas."

"Isn't Providence Island to the north of Haiti?"

"No," I explain, while scanning the table of contents. "It's the island where Nassau is situated. Actually, these days it's called New Providence."

I turn the pages, looking for the historical section. Joyce has moved closer and she is staring at me.

"What are you wearing around your neck?" she asks.

"A Nikolski compass."

"A *what?*" she presses, her hand reaching for the compass.

I don't know why, but I trust this girl. I put down the Bahamas guide and carefully untie the string from around my neck. But my hands are unsteady and the compass slips from my fingers. I don't yet fully realize what's happening, what is about to happen. I watch the compass drop in slow motion. There is a noise of shattering plastic as the casing breaks apart. The central sphere, freed from its shell, bounces on the floor, flies between Joyce's feet, spins across the living room pointing in all directions at once, and rolls down the gaping hot-air vent in the middle of the room.

I drop to my knees by the vent, just in time to hear the heart of the compass ricocheting more and more faintly against the metallic walls of the duct, until it gradually dwindles into silence far below.

The furnace takes this cue to start up and blow a scornful blast of air into my face.

The Beast

I OPEN THE CELLAR DOOR and flip the switch, but nothing happens. Another burnt-out light bulb. I have to feel my way along to the next switch. I hesitate to move into the dimness of the staircase. Every time I find myself in an enclosed space, I somehow end up having to deal with bizarre situations.

Joyce looks over my shoulder into the dark. I suggested she wait for me quietly with the teapot and the travel guides, but she insisted on coming along, on the pretext that if I left her alone for two minutes she would fall asleep.

I cautiously advance into the stairway. Behind me, Joyce counts the steps in a low voice. The staircase seems longer than usual. I feel as if we're diving twenty thousand leagues under the ground floor. The walls become covered with little spiral shells that I never noticed before, and after many minutes—"One hundred and thirty-five steps," Joyce specifies—the stairs disappear under inky water.

"Shit, the sump pump has broken down again! That's the second time this fall."

"Is the water very deep?" Joyce asks.

Probing farther, I take one step too many. I lose my footing, try to catch hold of the banister, hurtle down the remaining steps on my heels and plunge thigh-deep into the icy water. The cold and shock leave me breathless. I turn toward Joyce to inform her that we're going right back up to the apartment, but too late. She's come down to join me in the water, apparently impervious to the cold.

She greets my look of astonishment with a quick smile and a shrug.

"I know. I only came to borrow a travel guide. But"—she gestures toward the darkness—"there's no choice. We have to find your compass, right?"

What is there to say, now that both of us are standing in the freezing water? We plunge into the gloom, moving like deep-sea divers. I grope around for the light switch, but Joyce is one step ahead of me, and I hear her tug on the chain.

The light goes on—an old 20-watt bulb hanging from a stripped wire   and the Beast emerges from the darkness.

The furnace in our building frightens me in a way that is hard to account for. It is, after all, nothing but an ordinary oil furnace of the interwar period, massively corpulent, once painted white but now covered with scars and bumps. Through the grate, thin little strings of soot leak out into the water, and on its huge square brow a pair of screw holes form small, glowing eyes. The screws once fastened a brass plaque, which now lies at the foot of the furnace. Judging from the dust marks, the plaque has not been moved since I last looked at it, eight years ago.

Etched onto the brass plaque is the Beast's pedigree:

Manufactured in 1921 by

LEVI ATHAN & CO.

Nantucket, Massachusetts

Eight Januarys in this building have allowed me to observe with absolute precision the furnace's breathing habits. It always begins with a long sigh that then breaks up into a number of short sighs. It doles out about sixty of these sighs over a period of ten minutes, without hurrying, then dives once again into the depths. After an hour and a half of apnea, the cycle starts over again. This respiratory pattern is unchanging, whether the thermometer shows 5 or 55 degrees below zero. As a result, in the middle of winter, the interval between start-ups provides a good demonstration of the climate in northern Siberia.

I never thought that I would have to delve into furnace anatomy tonight. I sidle along the wall to investigate the situation more closely. Flames growl in the belly of the Beast, just a few centimetres from my nose. I would rather turn back, but I think of the Nikolski compass and keep going.

At the back of the machine, a dozen or so hot-air ducts going up toward the inhabited part of the building are intertwined in a complex intestinal network. One look is enough to convince me that a conscientious worker once riveted these tubes in place to last for centuries, thus condemning to a process of slow digestion any object that happened to drop down the air vents of the upper floors.

My whole body begins to shake. The burning proximity of the furnace does nothing to raise the temperature of the water we're standing in. I think of the steaming teapot three floors up. If we don't get out of here, we run the risk of hypothermia or pneumonia of the brain. I mumble a quick requiem for the compass and, with my legs gnawed away by the cold, start to climb out of this hole.

"My compass is a lost cause!" I announce dramatically.

Joyce seems not to have heard me. While I was examining the back of the furnace, she has been inspecting the rest of the cellar, as comfortable in standing in ice water as she was in my living room.

"Where does this go?" she asks, pointing to a padlocked door.

"Nowhere. That's my locker. And to think I have boxes in there. It must be crawling with crabs by now."

I find the key on my key ring and force it into the rusted lock. The door opens onto a half-dozen spongy cardboard boxes covered with purply urchins. I let out a downhearted sigh and, having ripped open a box, feel around inside with a certain sense of apprehension. My frozen hand recognizes the rough texture of a familiar object.

It's the old Three-Headed Book.

Distant Early Warning

OUTSIDE, THE STORM RAGES with even greater intensity. This is no time to go anywhere. I lend Joyce some dry clothes: a pair of jeans, an old sweater, woollen socks that don't match. We separate to get changed—the bathroom for her, the bedroom for me.

As soon as I'm dressed, I hurry to brew some more tea. When I come back to the living room with the teapot, Joyce is sitting on the couch, leafing through the Three-Headed Book. I'm startled for a second, disturbed by the sight of her wearing my things. She looks like my female double, some cousin just arrived from out of nowhere.

"Their names were Anne Bonny and Mary Read," she announces with a grin. "And you were right. When the English captured Jack Rackham's crew, they were the only ones to defend the ship."

"What happened then?"

"The English took the crew away to be tried in Jamaica. They were all hanged, all except for Bonny and Read, who were both pregnant. The English apparently didn't like to execute unborn human beings, so they threw them in prison while waiting for them to give birth. Mary Read died of a fever not long after."

"What about Anne Bonny?"

"Anne Bonny escaped and was never heard from again. Vanished into thin air. She may have returned to Providence to have her child."

I set the teapot down on the coffee table. At the very same moment, the furnace emits a long, provocative belch. For an instant I imagine the compass reappearing, carried aloft on a cloud of steam. I let out a sigh. Joyce closes the book and lays it down near the teapot.

"Don't you have anything stronger than tea?" she asks. "Your lips are still blue. You could use something with more kick to it."

After a quick visit to the kitchen, I put two small glasses on the table, along with a bottle of cheap Jamaican rum. "The hanged man's vintage," Joyce teases. I fill the glasses to the brim, we lift them in a silent toast and then, down the hatch. The alcohol instantly radiates through my veins.

"Was the compass very valuable?" Joyce asks as she sets her glass back down.

"Not really. It was a five-dollar compass made out of plastic, but it was from my father. He'd given it to me as a birthday present. I never knew my father, so the compass took on symbolic value for me."

"You never knew your father?"

"My parents met on the West Coast. When my mother became pregnant, she came back to live in the suburbs of Montreal. She exchanged letters with my father for some years, but I never saw him."

"Not even a photo?" Joyce wonders.

"The only photograph of him is hanging on the wall behind you, near the map of Puerto Rico."

Joyce gets up to examine the picture more closely. My mother is alone on a pebble beach, her hair ruffled by the sea breeze, visibly chilled to the bone in spite of her bulky down-filled military parka. Behind her, the landscape is littered with hundreds of bleached whale bones. A little farther back, one can just make out a metal-clad hut and, beside it, a short-wave radio antenna.

"Where's your father?" asks Joyce, frowning.

"You see that big blurry spot to the right? That's his finger sticking out over the lens. He was holding the camera."

Joyce quickly refills the glasses. Toast, down the hatch. I'm starting to feel the rolling waves.

"Did he stay on the West Coast?"

"Yeah. He went as far as Alaska, to a little village called Nikolski. For years, I thought every compass in the world was manufactured there. I pictured a huge compass factory built right at the North Pole. I had some strange ideas."

"Not at all," Joyce objects. "The magnetic north travels around. It may have moved through Nikolski, right?"

"An appealing theory, but Nikolski is too far south."

I go to get the cardboard tube where I keep my maps. After pushing the coffee table out of the way, I unfurl the maps on the floor, and anchor the corners with the bottle of rum, the teapot and two stacks of travel guides. Joyce kneels down beside me, which fills me with a dizziness I try to blame on the rum rather than the heady closeness of her knee to my hand.

The first map is of the Arctic Ocean.

"So. Right now, the magnetic north is located on Ellef Ringnes Island, here. It's gradually approaching the geographic North Pole. At the beginning of the century it was situated in the corner of Boothia Peninsula, almost two thousand kilometres to the south."

"And Nikolski?"

"It's on another map."

As I pull out the map of Alaska and place it on top, the teapot and bottle of rum come dangerously close to tipping over. Joyce catches the bottle and, while she's at it, refreshes our libations. Toast, down the hatch. The living room is starting to pitch.

"You see? Nikolski is on the island of Umnak, smack in the middle of the Aleutians—the archipelago shaped like a spinal column."

"Like a spinal column?" Joyce replies, sniffing the

bottom of her glass. "I always found the Aleutians resembled the West Indies."

Really? I open the guide to the Dominican Republic and juxtapose the map of the West Indies on that of the Aleutians. The second archipelago looks exactly like the first, but mischievously rotated through 180 degrees.

"So your father lived in Nikolski . . . ," she says, studying the map. "Talk about a hole."

"Thirty-six humans, five thousand sheep and a small crabmeat packing plant."

"What did he do there?"

"I have no idea. His letters weren't very clear. All I know is, he worked on a Distant Early Warning base."

"Distant Early Warning . . . I've heard of that somewhere."

"During the Cold War, the American army set up some sixty radar bases in the Arctic. The line started in Greenland, cut through the middle of the tundra and ended in Nikolski. It was called the Distant Early Warning Line. My mother put together a whole file on the subject: newspaper clippings, photos, old copies of *Life* magazine . . . Can't remember where I put it."

"Probably in the cellar, with the urchins."

"Probably."

"And how long did he stay in Nikolski?"

"He died there, not long after he arrived. They found him at the bottom of a platform on Christmas

Eve. The town doctor diagnosed a broken neck. The American army couldn't locate the family, so the body was buried there."

"So how did you find out?"

"His co-workers found a bundle of letters in his closet and they decided to write to each of the addresses to explain what had happened. They must have been hoping some distant nephew would ask for the body to be sent home. My mother answered, but her letter was returned to sender six months later. The U.S. Air Force had just shut down the base at Nikolski. I guess my father is still buried there, at the foot of a radar antenna."

"What about the other letters?" Joyce asks, pouring some more rum. "Do you know who they were from?"

I drain my glass with a grimace. "Who knows? My father was a sailor. Probably had a girl in every port—Hamburg, Shanghai, Callao . . . In which case I've got dozens of brothers and sisters scattered all over the planet. But I'll never know, because the letters have disappeared. They may have been burned, or chucked in a garbage dump, or buried with my father. Or maybe even classified Top Secret in the military archives of Anchorage."

Joyce lifts the bottle of rum from the corner of the map—which curls up slightly—fills the glasses, puts the bottle back and raises her glass ceremoniously.

"Well, then let's drink to the memory of your father, your mother, your scattered family and your old five-dollar compass, which valiantly kept pointing north until the very end."

I refrain from specifying that my compass did not point north but toward Nikolski—the story is already convoluted enough, thanks very much. We noisily slurp down our drinks and place the glasses back on the map, mine at Fairbanks and hers right in the middle of the Beaufort Sea. Well, that's it: I'm drunk, bowled over by the mixture of freezing water, childhood memories and cheap rum, not to mention Joyce's knee next to my hand.

I close my eyes and let myself sink headfirst into the Bering Sea.

Visa

AT FIRST GLANCE, the Burgos Lorenzo family library appears to be rooted in the house, as though it had embedded itself in the walls little by little over the centuries. On certain afternoons, when the light pours like gold through the windows, one can easily imagine a distant owner studying ponderous treatises on pearl cultivation, or Simón Bolívar drafting a fiery dispatch.

But this in fact is one of the house's many impostures. For the books actually arrived all at once, when Eduardo Burgos Lorenzo sold his properties in Caracas. The cargo—altogether some fifty massive wooden crates—was lowered into a ship's hold in the spring of 1977, unloaded at the Punta de Piedras dock, and then hauled to the top of the island with the help of three trucks and ten robust, underpaid islanders.

This commotion was an abiding source of amazement for the family. Why, after liquidating his houses without the slightest hint of sentimentality, was Eduardo Burgos Lorenzo so determined to hold on to this mound of books? Was he perhaps afraid of selling off a work that might eventually fetch a tidy sum? In spite of its size and the spectacular attention it received when it was moved, the library contained very little of great value. It was composed essentially of worthless theological monographs, outmoded military dissertations, outdated history textbooks, compilations of colonial poetry and anthologies of published authors, as well as an astonishing assortment of yellowed encyclopedias not recent enough to be useful as references but not old enough to qualify as antiques. It also housed a ravenous strain of mould, which swiftly took advantage of Margarita's maritime climate to flourish. Since then, billions of spores have been floating in the atmosphere of the house, like silent and malodorous witnesses to the library's strange journey.

255

The lesson of this story boils down to only one thing: Don Eduardo, who was never much of a reader, had quite simply overlooked the egregious insignificance of his books.

Noah is alone in the dark, sitting at the long mahogany table that divides the library in two. The antique copper reading lamp throws a circle of light around him. A bundle of tricoloured *Air Mail/Correo Aereo* envelopes, a strip of stamps bearing a marine tortoise design, and a road map of Saskatchewan are spread out within reach.

It has been raining constantly now for twelve days and twelve nights, as though a deluge threatened to swamp Margarita Island and disperse the passengers of this house to the four corners of the globe. Noah has shut himself up in the library with his letter-writing paraphernalia and, muttering the whole time, tries to ward off claustrophobia by blindly tossing the blue-and-red envelopes over the Canadian plains, as if involved in a vast game of naval warfare.

Bending over the road map, he performs an esoteric variety of algebra. The prairies are covered with hundreds of little circles, dates, postal codes, doodles and fingerprints. For years, Noah has recorded each letter with an x next to which he has scrawled when and from where the letter was sent. If a line were drawn connecting these x's in chronological order, it would reproduce his itinerary from 1989 through 1999, which took him from Saskatchewan to Montreal Island, from Montreal Island to Stevenson Island, and from Stevenson Island to Margarita Island, all of it superimposed (with the distortion this inevitably entails) on the curve of the Souris River, on the sprawl of Saskatoon and on the Chipewyan reservations.

"Am I disturbing you?"

Noah starts. Arizna has come into the library without a sound.

"I was writing a letter. You can come in. I'm almost done."

She walks over to the table, not saying a word. Noah has just chosen an address (Rouleau, Saskatchewan SOG 3V7) and hurriedly marks it on the envelope. This is the ninth letter to his mother this week, a direct result of the foul weather plaguing Margarita.

Arizna sits down facing him, on the opposite side of the table. She seems tired—that is, much more tired than usual.

Noah is concerned. "Are you okay?" he asks.

"So-so. I've received some bad news about my grandfather."

"What's the matter? Is he ill?"

"Ill? My grandfather? That would be a surprise. He's unsinkable, the old fox. No—he's disappeared."

"Disappeared?"

"The police have put out a warrant for his arrest. Something to do with a scam. I haven't been given the details yet. They raided his house this morning but they can't find him anywhere: not at home, not at his job, not at his country house."

"Who issued the warrant?"

"Warrants—there are a few: one from the Caracas police, another from the police in Miami and one from Interpol."

"That's odd. I would have thought the Chávez government might be more reluctant to help the Americans."

"There's a diplomatic truce. My grandfather worked for the consular services under Carlos Andrés

Pérez, so he has no support in the current government. But that's not all. Since he was the primary shareholder in Tortuga Publications, the police have threatened to search our offices, seize our computers and freeze the bank accounts. They could also cancel your visa, since you're our guest. And there's no guarantee they won't put me in custody, on the presumption that I might be hiding something."

"Shit . . ."

"My thoughts exactly. So the point is, I have a favour to ask of you. I'd like you to go spend Christmas in Montreal with Simón, until things settle down."

"No problem. When do we leave?"

"Around four a.m."

"Four a.m.?! Are you kidding me?"

"Not at all. I've already bought your tickets."

"But . . ."

"And, here, I've prepared this for you, too."

She hands him a Venezuelan passport and a small white envelope. The passport opens to a colour photograph of Simón. The boy is beaming, as if he were going to hunt for treasure at the beach, not confront the dreaded customs officers of North America.

Noah opens the envelope with some trepidation. What unfolds in his fingers is an official letter, written in three languages, in which Arizna Burgos Mendez, being sound in body and mind, designates Noah Riel as the biological father and legal guardian of Simón

Burgos, in witness whereof she signs hereunder at La Asunción (Nueva Esparta), Venezuela, on this 16th of December, 1999.

"I think," she explains, in an almost neutral tone of voice, "this will be enough to get you through customs."

259

All that can be heard in the library is the muffled patter of the rain against the windows. Noah nods his head. He is obviously dazed, but his face is lit up by a faint smile. Incredulous, he rereads the letter, folds it carefully and slips it back in the envelope. He says nothing   there is nothing to say. The silence lingers. Arizna wears a frown as she looks for some memorable phrase to close this chapter of her life.

"Go get your bags ready," she finally says. "I'll take care of Simón's."

She gets up and, with a little wave, fades into the shadows. Noah finds himself alone, holding Simón's passport. He smiles as he contemplates the photo. Then he leaps up from his chair, scoops up everything on the table   envelopes, stamps, Saskatchewan road maps—and sends the whole lot flying into the wastepaper basket in an avalanche of dust and paper.

He rubs his hands together, turns off the lamp and goes to pack.

Little Dipper

SOMEONE IS KNOCKING AT THE DOOR.

No answer. There's no sign of life in the apartment, except for the faint hum emanating from a black, rotary-dial telephone which, apparently, has been off the hook for a number of minutes. The old-fashioned instrument, splattered with countless flecks of white paint, seems to have been cut out of a starry sky. Five large white spots on the receiver reproduce the Little Dipper.

The telephone is poised on a stack of computer programming handbooks, next to an empty bottle of rum and an old clock showing 6:37 a.m. Pinned on the wall are two yellowed news clippings about the arrest and trial of a woman accused of piracy in the United States in 1989.

The desk is in a mind-boggling state of chaos. To all appearances, the drawers have been emptied and a number of objects gathered up during a hasty departure. An informed and thorough analysis of the scene would point to the absence of a notebook, a set of CD-

ROMs, a Spanish dictionary, an extensive supply of counterfeit cards and an old blue sailor's duffel bag.

Ruling over the disorder, in the middle of the room, sits a cathode ray monitor and a computer on which the name Louis-Olivier Gamache has been inscribed with a black felt pen. The computer is running (one can hear the unobtrusive purr of its cooling fan), and the messages on the screen indicate that the hard disk has just been erased and reformatted.

The condition of the rest of the room is much the same.

Strewn over the floor are a bowl containing remnants of crab-fried rice (topped with a pair of lacquered chopsticks), a pot redolent of codfish soup spiced with cumin, a tin of sardines emptied of its passengers, and a depleted bag of shrimp chips. The culinary trail leads to the sink, which is surrounded by an even greater jumble of dirty dishes. A kettle, a jar of tea bags and a teapot have been left high and dry on the stove.

At the southern end of the room, a sash window leads out to the fire escape. The window is wide open, despite the bad weather outside. The curtains wave gently and, on the floor, a puddle of melted snow is slowly spreading.

On the other side of the door someone is still knocking.

A God for Bluffers

THE NOISE OF A DIESEL ENGINE wakes me at seven in the morning.

I open an eye. I'm still stretched out on the living-room floor, with my head between the teapot and the bottle of cheap Jamaican rum. I have a Bukowski-style headache and an unpleasant impression of déjà vu.

I stumble over to the window and hang on to the bamboo curtain. Outside, the rain has stopped, and a fine snow is falling silently on the statue of Dante Alighieri, while a municipal snowplough rolls by, showering the street with salt and sparks.

Yawning, I reflect on where all that salt might very well come from. Probably from the Magdalen Islands. The salt cycle provides an outstanding illustration of the vanity of existence. Patiently deposited by the sea over millions of years, blasted out with dynamite, milled into grains, shipped out in cargo ships, loaded into the snowplough, spread throughout Montreal's arterial system, then finally washed down the sewers in the direction of the ocean whence it came.

How small we are.

The snowplough disappears at the corner of the street and I step away from the window. The living room is in the same condition it was in last night: the map of Alaska is still unfurled on the floor, held down by the teapot and the empty bottle of rum. The old Three-Headed Book is still lying there on the coffee table, along with a couple of grimy glasses and a split-open compass.

Nothing has budged, but the old sailor's duffel is gone, the yellow raincoat is gone, Joyce has shoved off.

Picking up the rum bottle, I shiver as I estimate the amount of alcohol that was polished off last night. I can feel my liver withering. Am I growing old? The fact is, I'm hardly in the habit of imbibing so unreservedly. I decide to go dissolve all of it in the shower.

Walking toward the bathroom, I instinctively sweep my eyes across the bookshelf, and do a double take. An unusual gap has opened up among the travel guides. My book thief has been at it again! I quickly identify the missing volume as the *Rough Guide to the Dominican Republic*.

Perplexed, I contemplate the gap as one might consider the missing piece of a puzzle. Those few centimetres of void sum up all I know about my book thief, which is next to nothing.

I'm still mulling over this meagre clue when I discover in the bathroom an old sweater and a still-damp pair of jeans. Joyce absconded without even taking the time to retrieve her clothes. An exit straight out of a cheap detective novel! Well, she certainly did not skimp on surprises. Searching through the jeans I discover:

- a few coins (total, 61 cents);
- the business card of the S.W. Gam Bookshop on the back of which I scribbled my address;
- a crumpled cash register receipt ("hamsan—1—$3.75");
- a Hydro-Québec bill addressed to Ms. Joyce Doucette, residing on Mozart Street.

I look at my watch. Two hours left before the bookstore is scheduled to open. I dress hurriedly, throw Joyce's clothing into an old plastic bag and jump into my winter boots.

I charge down the stairs four at a time, cross Dante Park without even saying hello to the old writer, shoot like a bullet past my favourite Italian café, just barely avoid running into the snowplough, and scamper up Casgrain Street with the plastic bag tucked under my arm like a rugby ball.

At the corner of Mozart and Casgrain, I stop for a moment to catch my breath.

The snow has transformed this otherwise familiar intersection into a ghost-town setting. A few cars go by with a muffled hissing sound. Hardly anyone around, and the shops have not yet opened. A woman presses her nose against the closed door of the Italian grocery. After a moment's hesitation, she crosses the street, walks past the red neon salmon of Poissonnerie Shanahan and scurries toward Jean-Talon market.

I tighten my scarf and scan the street addresses around me. I soon find Joyce's building and, parked directly in front of it, two RCMP cruisers.

I make an effort to calmly take stock of the situation. Presently, I manage to identify four vehicles: two standard patrol cars, an unmarked beige Malibu (given away by its VHF antenna) and a white van, not to mention a minivan from the *Journal de Montréal*. But not a policeman in sight.

Keep cool—it's possible there's no connection between Joyce's hasty departure and these police cars.

I walk up to the door hoping to discover the signs of some domestic drama—scarlet stains, suspicious smoke—but all I can see are the decorative lights loosely draped around an artificial Christmas wreath. In a corner of the hallway, a plastic Santa Claus blinks feebly and seems to be mocking the entire universe.

I check the Hydro-Québec bill one more time. There's no mistake—this is indeed where Joyce lives, apartment 34. I take a deep breath, push the glass door open and start up the stairway.

On the third floor, a reporter is half-heartedly questioning a stubbly-faced man—the janitor, judging from the heavy set of keys attached to his belt—while his photographer, cigarette butt wedged between his lips, takes some rapid-fire shots of the premises. I skirt around the little group (the janitor gives me an odd look) and continue down the corridor. The policeman on duty blocks my way in front of apartment 32.

"Where do you think you're going?" he asks sharply.

"To see a friend."

"Which apartment?"

"Number 35."

I say the number without thinking. A shiver travels up my spine. What if all these officers were here precisely to pay a visit to the occupant of apartment 35? My careless bluff might be the end of me. Luckily I've picked the right number, and the policeman deigns to stand aside, but not without taking a good look at my face.

The door to apartment 34 is ajar. As I walk by, I glimpse several officers busying themselves amid a bewildering mishmash: filthy dishes, electronic equipment, clothing, books, computers, CD-ROMs, shredded paper. Sitting at the desk, a technician is attempting to reboot the computer, while two underlings wearing white gloves pack the contents of the apartment into cardboard boxes.

Joyce is clearly not at home.

So I am no further ahead. Now, how am I going to get out of here?

I go to knock on the door of apartment 35, trying to come up with a story before the tenant opens the door. Nothing comes to mind. As I stand there waiting, the policeman watches me suspiciously. His gaze is fixed on my plastic bag as if it held, not Joyce's damp clothing, but a homemade nail bomb. I put on an innocent face, examining first the door (various bruises), then the ceiling (water stains) and the floor (unidentified brownish rings). After a time it becomes apparent that apartment 35 is providentially unoccupied.

There is a god for bluffers!

I backtrack under the wary eye of the policeman, and go back down the stairs gingerly and with bated breath. My heart rate returns to normal only once I am on the street again. I linger for a moment in front of the building, pressing the bundle of Joyce's clothes under my arm.

The snowplough comes back the other way, spitting salt across the road.

The General Unlikelihood
of the Situation

FLIGHT 502 TO NEWARK is due to leave Caracas at
7:10 a.m. local time.

Noah and Simón, who have just come in from
Margarita, have scarcely fifteen minutes to catch the
flight. The rain is hammering against the glass walls of
the national terminal, but there is no sign of any slow-
down in airport activity. At most, some flights are ten
minutes late. A few travellers, contorted in their plastic
chairs, sleep unperturbed. From time to time, flight
numbers are announced on the loudspeakers. Rum and
black coffee are both served, without distinction, at the
refreshment counter. The comforting routine of an
international airport.

Noah and Simón gallop through this great calm
and at the last minute locate their boarding gate. A
sleepy-eyed woman checks their tickets, pushes them
into the airplane and shuts the heavy hatchway
behind them.

At exactly 7:18 a.m., just as the old Boeing 727 rises from the runway, the airport notice boards start clacking in unison. All flights scheduled that day will be delayed for an unspecified period because of weather conditions.

Our two fliers are quite oblivious. They gain altitude, leave the airspace of Caracas, and climb through the cloud ceiling just in time to see the sun come up.

Simón takes the events with extraordinary composure. It is true, though, that the strangeness of their departure is tempered by the general unlikelihood of the situation. In a world where you cross the Caribbean at ten thousand metres above sea level while listening to Britney Spears on closed-circuit, what could be more natural than to decamp at two in the morning without telling anyone goodbye, in order to spend the winter holidays in the hemisphere next door?

Pressing his nose against the porthole, Simón silently marvels at the ice crystals. The on board thermometer indicates that the outside temperature is 40 degrees Celsius below zero, a figure that boggles the mind.

At the airport in Newark, they pass through customs without a hitch. The customs officer appears unfazed by the arrival of a half-Chipewyan father with his half-Venezuelan young son. Noah pockets the passports with a sigh of relief, and off they go to a new boarding gate, a new Boeing, a new adventure.

Terminal C looks like a refugee camp: hundreds of travellers everywhere, sitting on their luggage or on the floor. The sleet has grounded planes for hours, and an amorphous crowd is thronged at the counters of the international area. Noah studies the monitors. The next flight to Montreal is put off indefinitely. The end of the day seems more remote than ever.

They ensconce themselves in an unoccupied corner. Simón is philosophical about the holdup and busies himself studying every detail of the surrounding chaos. A few paces away, a monitor is broadcasting the CNN Airport Network non-stop.

Their closest neighbour is a young woman around thirty years old. She has short hair, an oversized sweater and slim reading glasses. She is seated nonchalantly on an old blue sailor's duffel bag and munches on chips as she leafs through a guidebook to the Dominican Republic.

Noah vaguely follows CNN, a blend of news and commercials interspersed with stock market figures. Simón and the girl sneak glances at each other. They appear to find each other intriguing—two birds perched side by side on an electrical wire. After a time, she half smiles and holds out the bag to him.

"Want some?"

Simón looks with distrust at these crunchy pinkish snacks. The label shows cryptic orange ideograms— nothing to help identify either the contents or the taste.

"Shrimp chips," she explains. "They're crazy about them in Japan. Do you know about Japan?"

"I know Pokémon!" Simón exclaims.

Reassured, he snaps up a chip and chomps at it enthusiastically. Over his head, Noah and the girl exchange a polite smile.

"Your son?" she asks.

He nods. Simón has another chip. Then, suddenly, the monitors start to flash. New departure times pop up beside various destinations. A huge sigh of relief goes through Terminal C as immediate boarding is announced for Chicago, London and Santo Domingo. The girl slips the guidebook into her pocket.

"I've got to go," she tells them as she rises to her feet. "Good luck!"

Simón waves to the girl, who moves off and vanishes, literally engulfed by the throng.

Noah's mind is on something else. A thread of sweat runs down his neck and goosebumps spread over his arms. On the television, there is a special report on the violent floods in Venezuela.

He tries to believe this is a mistake, but the caption over the pictures—*Flash Floods in Venezuela*—leaves no room for misinterpretation. A working-class district of Caracas has been sliced in half by a torrent of mud and debris. A series of headlines stream by over the NASDAQ indices. The death toll numbers in the thousands, and tens of thousands of houses have been destroyed.

Questions roll through Noah's head: Were there landslides in Margarita? Was Don Eduardo's house swept away? Are Arizna and Bernardo safe?

He shakes his head. Nothing that has happened today can match the unlikelihood of this flood, which came out of nowhere. After all, he and Simón went through Caracas just a few hours ago, and there was nothing to foreshadow a disaster such as this. All at once, he feels as though he has been travelling for much longer than is actually the case.

Simón tugs impatiently on his sleeve.

"What?" Noah asks.

"They just announced the plane for Montreal."

Noah comes back from his thoughts. He looks at the departures monitor. Clever kid—he's right. Their flight is scheduled to leave in twenty minutes at Gate C42—at the far end of the terminal. They grab their bags and dash off again.

A Small Circle

THE SHOPS CLOSED FOR THE NIGHT over an hour ago. It's dark, it's snowing, and with the Christmas lights arrayed on either side, Mozart Street looks like a deserted landing strip. At the corner of Casgrain, the salmon in Poissonnerie Shanahan's window manages to sputter on between gusts of wind, stubbornly swimming against the current of an imaginary river toward the spawning pool of its ancestors.

Huddled inside a telephone booth, Noah watches the mist rise from his mouth. The temperature is barely 5 degrees below zero, but never in his life has he felt this cold, except perhaps in a truck stop in southern Alberta on Christmas Night 1979, when the trailer's radiator gave up the ghost. He presses the frozen plastic of the receiver against his left ear. At the other end, he hears nothing but metallic clicks and crackling, and he begins to wonder whether he has dialed the wrong number. After a while the international operator's voice faintly pierces the interference.

"Hi-*bonsoir-comment-puis-je-vous-aider*-how-can-I-help-you?"

For a few seconds Noah is thrown off balance. The accent seems to be neither Québécois nor American nor Latin American, but a sort of amalgam originating in every place and no place at the same time, as if the voice did not really belong to a human being but to a spurt of DNA designed to meet a specific need and then injected into the circuits of the telephone system. An entity with no accent, no nationality and no trade-union demands.

"I'd like to make a collect call to Venezuela," Noah declares after a moment's hesitation.

"What is the number?"

He gives the regional code of Nueva Esparta and the number of the Burgos residence, while restlessly surveying the area around the phone booth. No visible movement, aside from the blowing snow and the flickering salmon at Shanahan's fish store. An agitated, diligent silence hovers at the other end of the line. One can just make out, in the background, the inconspicuous tapping of a keyboard, most likely a recording from which one is supposed to gather that international operators do indeed have fingers, and therefore bodies.

"I'm sorry," she finally says. "The line is down."

"You mean the person's telephone line has been cut?"

"No, service seems to have been disrupted throughout the whole region. Weather conditions are bad in Venezuela. The infrastructures may have been damaged. I advise you to call back a little later."

Noah says thank you and hangs up. He cautiously opens the door of the phone booth a crack, and adjusts his too-thin coat and his too-short scarf.

"*Carajo*," he swears, mechanically.

He turns his head in response to a rumbling noise. An unfriendly-looking snowplough is approaching from the intersection. It roars past him, comes to a halt amid a blast of salt and gravel and laboriously starts away again. Noah jumps over the ridge of snow and follows in the plough's wake.

When he arrives at the apartment, Maelo is watching the televised news bulletin. Set out on the table, so they cannot be missed, are a bottle of *mamajuana* and two small glasses. Noah shakes the snow from his coat and hangs it on the coat rack.

"Well?" Maelo asks as he opens the bottle.

Noah drops onto the couch and wriggles his toes to try to get the blood flowing again.

"No news. The lines are down. I'll go out to call again later."

On the screen, Hugo Chávez is declaring a state of emergency in the states of Vargas, Miranda, Zulia, Falcón, Yaracuy, Nueva Esparta and Carabobo, and in the federal district of Caracas. This is the most devastating flood to hit South America in decades.

"Are you worried about her?" Maelo asks Noah, as he proffers a glass of *mamajuana*. ✓

Noah dreamily whiffs the contents of the glass and shrugs. Images flash randomly across the screen. A river of mud flowing through a slum area. A small red car wedged into a concrete wall. A man thigh-deep in brownish water, holding a child in his arms. Helicopters, fire trucks, ambulances.

"No," Noah finally replies. "There's no reason to worry. It would take a volcanic eruption to budge the Burgos house. It's gigantic, with walls *this* thick. And built on the highest point in the city, near the Santa Rosa fort. It's the safest place on Margarita Island."

The General Assembly of the UN has replaced the turmoil of the floods on the television screen. They are deliberating on disarming Iraq, inspection teams, the demands of the United States.

The telephone rings. Maelo reaches for it and, without lowering the volume of the TV, answers a cautious "Hello?" A smile of relief spreads across his face. "Finally! I've been waiting to hear from you since this afternoon . . . Yes . . . What? Four hours at Newark airport?"

"Yeah, it was nuts in Newark," Noah puts in.

He uncaps the bottle of *mamajuana* and pours himself a good-sized glass. On the TV, the local weather forecast for the next few days is snow and sleet in abundance. He takes the remote control and switches channels. On every station, there is nothing but mud-slides, refugees and antitartar toothpaste.

"Yes," Maelo continues. "They came to the fish shop. Asked me tons of questions. I told them I didn't know anything . . . No idea. They emptied out the apartment. It took them nearly the whole day. Did you ever happen to do any cleaning from time to time? . . . *¡Chistosa!* . . . Hey, I have to let you go. I've got guests . . . Yes . . . Fine. Let me hear from you when you have a minute. And don't let Grandmother Úrsula make life too hard for you!"

He hangs up and grabs his glass of *mamajuana*.

"It's the season of hurried departures," he explains between two sips. "A friend of mine needed to take an emergency vacation. I sent her to get some sun at my grandmother's place."

Noah nods absent-mindedly. He drains his glass in one go and yawns slowly.

"Well, I'm going to bed. I'm wasted."

"Sweet dreams."

Noah totters over to the bedroom and opens the door very gently. The beam of light sweeps across the room and illuminates the capelins swimming on the wall. He shuts the door behind him, muffling the sound of the television.

"Noah?" a small voice whispers in the dark.

He sits down on the edge of the mattress and strokes Simón's forehead.

"What is it?"

"Can you tell me a story?"

"I already told you one earlier. Now it's time to sleep. Come on, shove over a bit."

A series of waves ripples through the sheets when Simón crawls over to the other side of the mattress. Noah shivers as he undresses, pulls on a dry pair of woollen socks and slides under the starfish. It's strange to be able to recognize the least little bump in the mattress, and to find the discomfort both familiar and reassuring.

"Good night," he mutters in Simón's direction.

"Good night."

He sinks his head into the pillow, closes his eyes and exhales blissfully. The room goes quiet. The sports news can be heard indistinctly through the wall.

"Is it true you lived here before?" Simón asks.

"Hmmm," Noah confirms. "I lived with Maelo for four years."

He lets out a long yawn. On the other side of the wall, a sports analyst discusses injuries, power plays and penalties.

"And this was your room?" Simón insists.

"This was my room," Noah sighs, trying very hard to hold on to sleep.

"So this, this is the bed you slept in!"

"This is the bed I slept in . . ."

. . . *back when I was allowed to sleep*, he thinks, unfairly. In reality, there were many more reasons for insomnia back then, and Noah can easily recall all the wakeful nights he spent inside these walls: the nights he spent studying, the heat-wave nights, the *jututo* nights that went on until the neighbours called the police, the nights he wrote letters to his mother, the nights spent with road maps trying to guess where his mother was, the nights he doubted his mother existed, the end-of-term nights (dark and dreamless), the anxious nights, the epidemic nights, the nights thinking about his father, the nights when he tried to picture Nikolski, the nights spent wearing a bathrobe and lying in bed with a bottle of acetaminophen and a glass of water, the novel-reading nights, not to mention the nights with Arizna, those fleeting episodes that disrupted forever the peaceful course of his life.

Simón does not ask any more questions. He stares at the ceiling and says nothing, as if he too were pondering those long-ago nights, the distant echo from before his birth. How can so many memories be contained in such a cramped room? He raises his arm and traces a little circle, as though wanting to circumscribe his father's whole life.

"But it *really is so small*," he breathes into Noah's ear, his voice full of wonder.

Noah sits up halfway. It takes a few seconds for him to realize that Simón is referring to the bedroom. He smiles and kisses his forehead.

"You'll see. You'll get used to it before long."

Clearance

ONLY TWO DAYS LEFT BEFORE CHRISTMAS, and eight before the end of the world.

The bookstore has been almost deserted for a week. People are scurrying around elsewhere—anywhere it glitters, in the mazes of plastic and stainless steel, the china shops, the Pac-Man outlets, the luxury perfume stores, the poultry slaughterhouses. The used-book market is nosediving in the city and, frankly, I don't care very much. I've just finished making a sign, which I've placed on the counter right next to the cash register:

S.W. GAM BOOKSHOP

SEEKS

EXPERIENCED CLERK

FULL OR PART-TIME

NOMADS NEED NOT APPLY.

I rub my hands as I examine the sign. Well, that's done. Mme Dubeau, my esteemed proprietor, has been urging me for several days to prepare the job offer and put it up. She seems to be afraid I'll leave without warning, and let the bookstore fall entirely on her shoulders.

The truth is, I've been preoccupied of late.

All my free time (including a significant portion of my daily schedule normally earmarked for sleep) has been devoted to clearing out my apartment. I've been sorting old, inert objects, dusting them off one by one and propelling them into a new life. Furniture and dishes to the Salvation Army. Idiotic knick-knacks to the antique dealers. Assorted articles—sound system, bead curtains, desk lamp, floor lamp, chandeliers, pétanque balls, artificial Christmas tree, ladder—to the flea market. I'm entrusting the bamboo plants, spider plant and papyrus to my neighbour. The old income tax reports and government papers to the recycling bin. The rest—unclassifiable and unsalvageable—I unceremoniously cram into ultrastrong plastic bags for the garbagemen's enjoyment.

My books are naturally entitled to special treatment. I've hermetically wrapped the most valuable ones and stored them in the basement, in the notorious urchinridden locker, and I've brought the others here to be sold off at a dollar a piece.

Because of all this upheaval I make stupid errors. I make mistakes when totalling up prices, I completely mix up the titles when classifying books, and I neglect to watch for shoplifters, feeling that, in any case, the only book thief worth anyone's attention won't be back here again. Truth to tell, it did take me a few days to arrive at that conclusion. It didn't matter that I had come upon two RCMP squads in the process of search-

ing her apartment—I still held on to the slim hope that Joyce would not leave Montreal. I scrutinized the newspapers, trying to learn the reasons for the search, but there was no mention of it. The deskmen apparently did not think it warranted a headline, no doubt because the protagonist was still on the lam. As for me, I waited for her to show up at the bookstore sporting sunglasses and a blue wig.

The days went by. Hemmed in by the December frost, I quickly came back to the only scenario that made any sense. Joyce, evidently, was sitting pretty under a coconut tree, with her feet in the warm sand and a glass of *añejo* rum in her hand.

I've therefore decided to do something with my life. It's high time to escape from the gravitational pull of books. I will go without a guidebook, without an ency-clopedia, without a leaflet, without a phrasebook, with-out a schedule and without a road map. Occasionally I look at the shelves and sigh. I'll of course miss the bookstore a little, but it's more important for me to find my own road, my own little providence.

Jangle of the doorbell and icy gust of wind. A man and a child come into the bookstore. The man is wear-ing a plaid fall jacket and his teeth are chattering, and the child is swathed in three layers of wool and scarves. They shake the snow from their shoes and unbutton their coats. They are enveloped in a delicate aroma of charcoal, caramelized meat and cloves. They've undoubtedly just come out of Dunkel's, the Jewish delicatessen across the street.

While the little boy ventures toward the bookshelves as cautiously as a Sioux hunter, the man steps up to the counter. I notice him eyeing our job offer in a peculiar way.

"Interested?" I ask.

He shakes his head, but I feel inclined not to let the matter drop, as if, for some mysterious reason, I were convinced this man would be perfect for the position.

"You're wrong, you know. It's an ideal job: low wages but lots of time to read."

"I'll think about it," he answers with a smile. "In the meantime, do you have any books on dinosaurs?"

"A whole collection! Look at the end of the third row, under the blinking fluorescent light."

No need to repeat the information—the child has already scampered over to the third row. The man, meanwhile, lingers at the front of the shop. He scans the shelves, hovers for a moment over the "New Arrivals" table, glances at the Mickey Spillane shelf, and finally leans down to examine the cardboard boxes holding books I'm selling off for a dollar each. Most of what's jammed in those boxes is worth far more. One immediately discovers, for instance, three relatively recent travel guides (Indonesia, Iceland, Hawaii), an almost spotless copy of a Tintin book (*The Red Sea Sharks*), the *Ashley Book of Knots* (in good condition despite its missing cover) and a special edition of Georges Perec's *La Vie mode d'emploi* (luxury binding).

Squatting by the boxes, the man examines the books, turns them over, pushes them aside to see what's underneath. All at once I see him stiffen, as though he'd just stumbled upon a large, shrivelled-up tarantula at the bottom of the box. I quietly step closer. He is holding the old Three-Headed Book.

"Don't be fooled by appearances—what you have there is a unicum."

"Excuse me?" he says, as though emerging from a dream.

"A unicum. A book of which there is only a single known copy in the whole world."

"Really? How can you be so sure?"

"Look at it closely. It's made up of fragments of three books. The first third is from a study on treasure hunting. The second comes from a historical treatise on the pirates of the Caribbean. The final third is taken from a biography of Alexander Selkirk, who was shipwrecked on a Pacific island."

"So it's an anthology."

"No. These are fragments—literally. Debris. Flotsam and jetsam. The bookbinder salvaged the wreckage of three books and sewed them together. It's a piece of craftsmanship, not a mass-printed object."

The man turns the book over and over in his hands, like a Rubik's cube.

"That's weird. I don't understand why a book-binder would have done that."

"Hard to tell. A passion for puzzles, maybe . . . Look, I'll let you have it for fifty cents, employee discount."

Before he has time to respond, the child bursts out of the third row, his arms overflowing with treasures. The man lays the Three-Headed Book on the counter so that he can look at what the youngster has selected. I expect him to drastically reduce this copious selection, but no. He is content to read off the titles, approving each one with a satisfied nod of the head.

"*The Extinction of the Dinosaurs, The Time of the Saurians, The Great Fossil Guide, Giant Gallinaceans of the Jurassic Period* and *The Cretaceous Period As If You Were There.* Not bad at all. Nothing on hummingbirds?"

"Nothing on hummingbirds," the child answers, spreading his arms.

"Oh well, too bad."

He pushes the books toward me, puts two twenty-dollar bills on top of them and starts to button up the child's coat. I add up the price, discreetly giving him a 15 per cent discount, and wrap the purchase in an old plastic bag. When I hand him his change, the man smiles mysteriously.

"You know, your unicum. There's something missing."

I raise a quizzical eyebrow. By way of reply, he takes out of his wallet a small sheet of paper folded twice over and places it delicately on the Three-Headed Book. His forefinger stays on the paper for a moment, wavering. Then everything happens very quickly. He collects his bag, straightens his tuque and pushes the child toward the door, while wishing me Merry Christmas.

"*¡Feliz Navidad!*" the child adds, waving his mittens.

Jangle of the doorbell and a brief gust of frozen air. They've fled like two saboteurs who've just planted a time bomb.

Intrigued, I unfold the little sheet of paper. It's a map of the Caribbean, rectangular, about twenty centimetres long, bearing no date, no specific information. Nothing on the reverse side either. But there are various clues suggesting that it was made some time ago: the brittle grain of the paper, the yellowish oxidation, the tiny marks caused by fungus, the faded ink and the use of an archaic place name—British Honduras instead of Belize.

One of the sides of the map is roughly torn, as though it has been ripped out of an atlas.

I look toward the exit. The bell is still swaying back and forth over the door. Why did the man rush off like that? Was there some dark secret he was afraid would be brought to light? His words come back to me: . . . *your unicum. There's something missing.*

I bring the map closer to the Three-Headed Book, like the last remaining piece of a puzzle. My hunch is correct. The tear fits the binding exactly! This map, then, was torn out of the book some years ago . . . I stand there open-mouthed, contemplating the implications of this strange puzzle. Here is a discovery that clouds the issue rather than clarifying it.

Nothing is perfect.

I smile, shrug my shoulders and, after taping the map of the Caribbean into place, return the Three-Headed Book to the clearance box.

ACKNOWLEDGMENTS

The author: I would like to express my appreciation to Brigitte Malenfant and Francine Royer for acquainting me at the right time with the residency programme of the Conseil des arts et des lettres du Québec (CALQ), to Viviane Paradis and Josée Dubeau, who showed no pity in reviewing my grant applications, and to the team at the Internationales Künstlerhaus Villa Concordia, who made it possible for me to enjoy excellent working conditions.

A number of readers were patient enough to tackle this book in one or another of its many draft versions: Martin Beaulieu, Héloïse Duhaime, Sébastien Harvey, Saleema Hutchinson, Richard Levesque, Monik Richard, Antoine Tanguay, Hugo Tremblay, Bernard and Marie Wright-Laflamme, Viviane Paradis and Viriginie Rompré. Their comments allowed me to avoid numerous stumbling blocks.

I am grateful to Manuel Pimentel and Rossio Motta for making me aware of the *jututo*, to Joëlle Reid, for reminding me of her ancestor, and to Esther Cayouette, for checking certain parts of this story against reality.

For the English-language edition, I would like to thank Lazer Lederhendler and my editor at Knopf Canada, Pamela Murray.

Lastly, I must especially thank my family, my friends and my girlfriend for their support and wonderful patience during my writing marathons.

The translator acknowledges the assistance of the Banff International Literary Translation Centre (BILTC) at the The Banff Centre in Banff, Alberta, Canada. He would also like to thank the Collège international des traducteurs littéraires (CITL) in Arles (France), where this translation got underway, as well as the Canada Council for the Arts for providing a travel grant.

NICOLAS DICKNER won two literary awards for his first published work, the short story collection *L'encyclopédie du petit cercle*. Born in Rivière-du-Loup, Quebec, he travelled extensively in Europe and Latin America before settling in Montreal.

LAZER LEDERHENDLER is a three-time finalist for the Governor General's Literary Award, most recently for his translation of *The Immaculate Conception* by Gaétan Soucy, which was also shortlisted for the 2006 Scotiabank Giller Prize. He lives in Montreal.

A NOTE ABOUT THE TYPE

Pierre Simon Fournier *le jeune*, who designed the type used for the principal text of this book, was both an originator and a collector of types. His services to the art of print communication were his design of individual characters, his creation of ornaments and initials and his standardization of type sizes. Fournier types are old style in character and sharply cut. In 1764 and 1766 he published his *Manuel typographique*, a treatise on the history of French types and printing, on typefounding in all its details, and on what many consider his most important contribution to the printed word—the measurement of type by the point system.

BOOK DESIGN BY CS RICHARDSON